Winter Wife

Jessica Auerbach

*

"Winter Wife"

*

FK

*

Ticknor & Fields
New Haven and New York
1983

Library of Congress Cataloging in Publication Data

Auerbach, Jessica.
  Winter wife.

  I. Title.
PS3551.U384W5 1983   813'.54   83-5079
ISBN 0-89919-194-0

Printed in the United States of America

S   10 9 8 7 6 5 4 3 2 1

To Josh — for acts of faith.

There's a certain Slant of light,
Winter Afternoons—
That oppresses, like the Heft
Of Cathedral Tunes—

Heavenly Hurt, it gives us—
We can find no scar,
But internal difference,
Where the Meanings, are—

None may teach it—any—
'Tis the Seal Despair—
An imperial affliction
Sent us of the Air—

When it comes, the Landscape listens—
Shadows—hold their breath—
When it goes, 'tis like the Distance
On the look of Death—

Emily Dickinson

Winter Wife

One

$\int$HE supposed the new snow slowed him down. It was past twelve-thirty already.

The baby was crying again. She had to put Marissa down, put her in the carriage and push her to some far corner of the apartment — as if there were one, now that every inch was packed with changing table, stroller, diapers and all other imaginable baby equipment. Or slide her into a drawer and slam it shut.

"You're dry," Amy told the baby firmly. "You're fed." Marissa responded with the same undifferentiated accusation. "Please," she begged the infant, "please stop." Amy held her high on her shoulder. She had rubbed, patted, and finally thumped the baby's back over the last fifteen minutes. "All right, all right," Amy said, her voice quiet and carefully precise. "I don't know what else to do." She placed Marissa face down in the carriage and tucked a yellow hand-knit blanket tightly round her. "They like to be wrapped up like mummies," the hospital nurse had told her. "Makes them feel secure after they've lost their little home in the womb." While the baby rubbed her face back and forth against

the flannel sheet, Amy pulled the curtain across the hallway where
Marissa slept and ran for her own bed.

The second hand on the night table clock crawled round the
circumference of the dial while Marissa's cry grew sharper and
sharper. Amy breathed slowly, deeply, and closed her eyes. Timing
it this way, concentrating like this, helped, if only just a bit. She
breathed rhythmically in counterpoint to Marissa's cry. How old,
she wondered, are babies when they stop crying? At one o'clock
the sharpness eased and the pauses began. Amy measured these
pauses, heard them expand and separate the cries further and further from one another. Marissa was silent for thirty seconds, then
began again, but it was more subdued now, decidedly less persistent. Finally there was silence. Amy sat unmoving, waiting for the
next cycle. It did not come. She inhaled deeply. Less than half an
hour. Much better than yesterday. Now I'll rest, she thought, and
she wrapped her old grey cardigan round herself. She had stretched
the sweater badly during pregnancy, straining it further and further
each week across her expanding belly. Paul had started calling it
her "fat sweater." There was nothing as warm as that sweater, she
thought as she overlapped it across her chest. Ugly and warm.
Cozy for naps.

With so much snow, she thought, he couldn't be expected to
come. All that business of "neither sleet nor snow" was just catchy
phrasing. When the weather got bad enough, everything stopped.
Even here, she suspected, even out here in Minnesota. He had
never delivered packages every single day. Was it becoming less
and less frequent? Probably not. It was just that it had never been
every day.

When the doorbell rang, she had already drifted into sleep. She
froze, listening for Marissa's startle reaction. No baby noises. Had
she hesitated too long after the ring? Had he already climbed back
into his truck, packages and all? She mustn't run, now, mustn't
risk banging and bumping into things, for that would surely wake

Marissa. She brushed along the baby's curtain-sheet and on into the living room.

"She's asleep, isn't she?" the mailman asked as soon as she opened the door to him.

"I hope so," she said, glancing backward toward Marissa's nest.

"I'm sorry," he said, now in a whisper. The cold air rushed at her, racing into the living room beyond. "Would it be better if I knocked next time?" he asked. Would she hear a knock, she wondered, would she miss the delivery altogether if she told him not to ring? Would she find only "attempt to deliver" notices from now on? She wrapped her fat sweater more tightly round her. She wished she had remembered to take it off, wished she did not look like such a rag.

"Now I'm freezing you out, besides," he said. "You go back in and get warm again. You mustn't get chilled. That baby doesn't need a sick mother, that's for sure." He held two parcels wrapped in brown paper out toward her. "You've two today," he said. One was crushed, the outer paper ripped, the ragged baby-motif wrapping paper jutting out the open side. "You've a lot of relatives, don't you?" he asked. "I mean, there are a lot of presents."

"I didn't expect them." I didn't ask for them, she wanted to add. People didn't have to send them. They might have waited till things were going smoother, till she — well, deserved them more.

"People like babies," he said and smiled. She concentrated on the snow on his boots. A lot of snow, she thought, and our walk not even shoveled. "People send presents when there's a new baby," he continued. "It's nice for me, too, you know, coming to the same house every day. Being on a truck, you never get to know people. No neighborhood. Today I thought, maybe I'll just bring her one today and one tomorrow and get to deliver twice that way, but of course I couldn't. I don't mess with the law." He laughed softly.

"Listen," he said, and he had started to narrow the door opening. "I don't want you to worry about the bell waking her or any-thing." He glanced suddenly toward the street. They both watched the snow swirling in the light wind. "Does she have a schedule or something? I mean, can I maybe come earlier and she'll be awake?"

Amy shook her head. "She's just not a baby with a schedule, I guess. I feed her when she's hungry. Then I try to get her to sleep. She seemed to resist going down more the last few days."

He nodded. "What if I knock?" he asked. "Will you hear a knock?" She shrugged. She honestly didn't know. "I'll come a little earlier tomorrow." She turned the ripped package around slowly in her hands, then pulled the curly pink ribbon through the opening. She ran the ribbon through her fingers, curling it tighter against her thumb nail, watching it bounce back from her fingers when she released it. "I'll take off so you can get warm again," he said, "but I want you to promise you won't rush to answer the door. I worry you might be bathing her or changing her. I don't want you to leave her any place unsafe. I'll wait. Promise you'll take your time."

"I promise," she whispered.

"Well, then," he said, "back to the cold." He raised his hand to his forehead in a salute. "And you," he said almost sternly, point-ing his finger at her, "you go wrap yourself in an afghan for twenty minutes and warm up, my dear." He started to pull the door closed, then stuck his head back in and added, "I'll see you tomorrow, I hope."

Amy had to lean and push into the door to get it closed firmly against the wind. There was a light coating of snow scattered through the foyer of the three-family house. There were enough old-house cracks to ensure that the snow would be preserved in its white, frozen state.

How did he stand the cold all those long hours in the truck? Ought she to have invited him in? Suggested he close the door behind him while they talked in the foyer, so at least then he wouldn't have had the wind hitting so fiercely at him? Should she have offered him a chance to sit down for a minute in the warm house? What might she have said? "A little hot chocolate . . . Joe?" She had no notion of his name, but now Joe popped into her head. She had no cocoa. And she had no cookies, cake — nothing. "Come in and have some . . . toast?" One couldn't offer toast. When would she bake? Twice that week she hadn't eaten lunch because she was always tending to the baby. There was no time, and then, when Marissa finally did go to sleep, all she wanted to do was sleep herself, or lie down, anyway, certainly not stand around the kitchen preparing lunch. A white-meat turkey sandwich on Jewish rye, that's what she wanted. If she could call a deli and have them deliver it — what heaven. And roast beef on Tuesday, pastrami on Wednesday, corned beef Thursday. She'd settle for tuna on a hard roll on Friday.

He had never come on a Saturday. He'd been coming for weeks, but never Saturdays. She supposed that meant he might be older than she had thought — old enough to have the special fringe benefit of weekends off. He came to the house three or four times a week, yet when she tried to imagine him, the blue grey of his parka with its Post Office insignia on the sleeve dominated the vision. He had no pack on his shoulder, for he was the truck man, delivering packages only. He wasn't as young as she, there was no question of that. Sometimes in the really bad weather, like today, he had his parka hood up and a blue knitted watch cap under it, too. She couldn't see his hair, its color or quantity. Old enough to be her father? Unlikely. She'd invite him in if it snowed again, or at least meet his glance more directly tomorrow. It was a brutally cold winter.

She returned to the bedroom with the packages. One came from her aunt in Baltimore, the other from a distant relative of Paul's in Arizona — someone she had never met and probably never would meet. Paul, in fact, had probably never met him either. It embarrassed her. The birth announcements had gone out to so many people. And now the obligatory little packages were flowing in, five and six a week, and she would have to write the empty-phrased thank-you notes to strangers. If she ever had another child, she would not send birth announcements. It represented the height of acquisitiveness, she now realized. The first package contained a tiny pink-flowered dress. She pushed it aside. The next held a blue tailored sunsuit. Clearly a boy's style. Must have been on sale, she thought. Marissa would never get to wear it. Save it for the next one, she could hear Paul saying. She pushed the box off the bed. Why not wait till Marissa was older, till she wore jeans and tee shirts and could get some use out of real clothes? Perhaps Marissa would never be older. Does a creature who can't even keep down half her breast milk ever grow big enough to stand, to talk, to wear jeans? She retrieved the sunsuit from the floor and folded the two tiny pieces of clothing neatly, put the cards with pictures of chubby pink-cheeked babies inside their corresponding outfits and placed them on Paul's bureau.

She turned on the television. Two faces popped into view. A man and a woman very close up. How intense they were! She had promised Paul she wouldn't watch TV in the afternoon anymore. She turned down the sound and sat at the end of the bed watching David berate Mona. David raised his hand to her, and, with a look of horror, Mona fled the room. The camera panned in on his face, all bitterness and hostility. Suddenly there was a cut to a panty hose commercial. Mona would never win, for she was a good character, destined to suffer long and hard at the hands of the evil characters. No subtle neurotic dissatisfactions quietly wearing away at marriage, here. This was bigger stuff: full-blown psychopaths wielding their terrible powers (and real deadly weapons, in some cases) over their weaker, submissive partners. David was relentless. He would never divorce Mona, even though he had another woman. He was a first-class bad guy, to be sure, but why was he so adamantly opposed to divorce? Perhaps Mona had money. David had a criminal record, but Mona didn't know about that, apparently. Amy had never figured out how Mona and David had ever ended up married to one another; that had all happened before Marissa's birth. She imagined that Mona had been pregnant, and that David, perhaps in an unusual surge of humanity, had married her. (To atone for having previously raped her?) Mona must have miscarried, and then there they were, horribly bound together, ad infinitum, "till death do us part" hanging ominously over Mona's head. Mona was in love with Etan. Amy turned it off. Two nights previously, after Paul had enumerated all the events and communications of his day, she had said, "Diana had a miscarriage." She had barely finished saying it when she realized what she was doing. She also realized she had been waiting to tell him while he told his news. Eager, anxious to share her own news. "Diana who?" he had asked her. She had laughed, trying to cover her lapse into unreality.

"On the soapies," she said. "A joke. I watched for five minutes while I nursed. Not much going on other than that, I guess." He had said nothing for a long while but had adopted an expression very similar to Steve's when he had heard that Eva had gone back to the streets that afternoon.

"Don't watch those anymore." She laughed again, shrugged.

"Promise?" he'd asked.

"OK," she had agreed, but she had felt angry, angry enough to walk out of the room, although she hadn't.

"Listen to the radio," he'd said.

It's the faces, she had wanted to say, but thought better of it and nodded.

"Any new gifts?" Paul asked when he came in the door. She sat on the bed while he read through the cards and took the tiny outfits from their gift boxes. "She can't wear the sunsuit," Amy told him.

"There's nothing wrong with the sunsuit," he said.

"Everyone'll think she's a boy," Amy said.

"She's a baby. What difference does it make?"

"It embarrasses everybody. The little old lady in the supermarket says, 'My word, what a handsome little boy you've got. All boy, he is, so strong-looking. What a good quarterback he'll make.' Then you correct her, in respect and deference to Marissa, who can't do it herself, and the old lady nearly has a heart attack. 'Oh dear, you just can't tell them apart these days. I'm so sorry, she is so darling, so delicate. You ought to put her in pink.'"

"If you don't want to put it on her, don't. She's got enough clothes without that, doesn't she?"

"Yes. But it's wasteful. All these clothes, and she'll never wear half of them. She wears undershirts and nightgowns all the time."

"They'll be too warm in summer."

She glanced toward the window. When it was dark outside, it was impossible to tell how high the ice came up on the window. Paul walked into the kitchen, paced it as though measuring its length and then double- and triple-checking his findings.

"You seem to have forgotten dinner," he said quietly. He had settled on that phrase only recently. Before that he had tried a more jolly, "What's for dinner?" and then, "Did you do anything about dinner?" Lately, though, he had lapsed into this "forgotten" idiom. Amy thought he meant it kindly. The sort of thing one said to protect the psyche of a three-year-old who has "forgotten" to go to the bathroom and has, instead, wet the new carpet at a crabby old relative's house. Paul wasn't mean.

And anyway, it was an accurate-enough appraisal. She had forgotten dinner. Forgotten it for weeks. Or was it months, now, stretching back into pregnancy days, as well? It was so easy to forget now. Her life was no longer neatly divided between night and day. Marissa cried when she wanted to, in darkness and in light. The days blurred together, punctuated only by short alternations of waking and sleeping. But it wasn't her fault. It was Marissa's fault. She was the one who had created the chaos. Perhaps, Amy could resist — stay awake during the day, sleep only at night, as she had done before, as most people did — but the fatigue in between feedings was very compelling. And Marissa's call continued to chop night sleep into tiny disconnected segments.

Did he say, "You seem to have forgotten dinner," now because he wanted to leave open the possibility that she might not have forgotten? It was a gentle accusation, but an accusation, nonetheless. "You," it began, "You have failed." Perhaps they would evolve to some higher level one day, like "What shall we do for dinner tonight?" There is no dinner, Paul, don't you know by now? He opened cabinets randomly, or so it seemed to her. "What do you want to do?" he asked. "You," again, she noted.

"Eggs?" she ventured.

"I hate eggs."

"You like omelets."

"I used to. We've had them too much lately."

"What, then?" He had a way of putting two fingertips to his forehead when tension escalated. She sighed as he did it now. She read in the elegant spareness of his gesture a simple warning: if things get any worse, I will bury my face, my whole face, not just my forehead, in my whole hands. Act now and save yourself a scene, she heard his fingertips admonish. "OK," she said, "there's a recipe for eggs in the *New York Times Cook Book*," and an ancient image of an elegantly prepared dish topped with chopped parsley floated into her consciousness. "We had it once a couple of years ago. You remember, you slice the eggs and add potatoes or something. It doesn't even taste like eggs. I could find it." She had pulled the book from its shelf and was riffling through the pages. "You remember it?"

"No."

"You liked it, I think. A sauce, like a white sauce, it had. Here it is," she said, passing him the book.

"We've only got five eggs," he said.

"We'll make it a bit smaller, that's all."

"Do you have potatoes?" She opened a lower cabinet and peered in. She turned and sat on the floor, leaning against the cabinet door. "You win," she said, "no potatoes."

"It's not a contest, Amy." It was his weary face that he now put on. Not tired. There was a difference. Not pitying, either. Just finely distilled impatience.

"You could have gotten potatoes," she said.

"I didn't know you had a potato dish planned. If you had mentioned it, I could have picked them up on the way home. Now everything that's in reasonable distance is closed."

"We can't have it without potatoes, I don't suppose?"

"No."

"Pizza from the place that delivers?" she suggested. He reached for the telephone book. She tried to remember how dinners used to be. There were ideas ahead of time, then. She used to take things from the freezer in the mornings, purchase missing recipe ingredients and side trimmings in the afternoons. That was a different life.

One of the magazines Paul had brought to her in the hospital had had an article entitled, "Menu planning for twenty-one days." A woman in Fargo did all her shopping for three weeks in one trip. Amy envisioned cart after cart of supermarket items, one pushed by her, one by Paul, a third and a fourth manned by hired help. They might pass Marissa back and forth amongst them, jiggling her up and down as she cried at the checkout.

After dinner, Paul got the baby when she cried. Amy could hear him talking to Marissa while he changed her. Little baby noises that he put on for the occasion. It made her uncomfortable to hear him do that. And he called her Rissy. A lot of sibilance and cooing. Amy never called her anything. It seemed silly. What did a baby care what you called it? It was like talking to a stuffed animal, almost. Later, when she was older, it would be entirely different. And hadn't they chosen the name *Marissa* because they liked its elegant sound, and because it wouldn't automatically be shortened by friends and teachers to a cutesy nickname?

"Have you thought anymore about weaning her?" he asked as he handed Amy the baby. She shook her head. "If you weaned her, I could be the one feeding her now." After a pause, he added, "I'd like to be able to do that."

"It's so much better for them to be nursed than formula-fed," she said. "And I won't do it forever, you know. You'll get to do all the solid food when that starts." If she were to stop nursing, there'd be the bottles, nipples, and formula. Every time the baby cried, there'd be a bottle to prepare and heat. And the issue of cleanliness. Babies died of diarrhea at this age. How could she risk it? What if she contaminated the formula? And God knows, in Minneapolis your life better not be dependent on anything that comes out of a grocery in the winter.

"Maybe you wouldn't be so tired all the time if you weren't nursing," he suggested.

"At least we won't run out of breast milk," she said. "I think that's awfully important, don't you?" She thought he nodded slightly.

Two

$\mathcal{A}$ MY had been five months pregnant when they moved to Minneapolis. She had sat on the couch (which hadn't been put in place yet but stood in the middle of the living room) while Paul unpacked everything. "I could really help," she had protested, but he said he didn't want her to exhaust herself. The drive out had been more than enough strain right then. Later, they moved to the kitchen and she watched him filling cabinets and shelves.

"No reason you can't use the backyard," the agent had told them, so after most of the boxes were emptied, they walked to the market nearby and bought a box of chocolate-covered doughnuts and a quart of milk. Then they took one of the blankets they'd used for packing and made a little picnic in the backyard. They broke their doughnuts in half and dunked them deeply into their mugs of milk. She watched the ripples of hot air waving above the paved driveway. This intense, close heat was a surprise — she had expected cool weather and had bought no maternity sundresses, no maternity shorts. "You like the house, don't you?" Paul asked in between sucks at his doughnut. Of course she did. It wasn't really that different from the apartment they'd had in New Haven, which was why they'd been attracted to it in the first place. And it had a modernized bath. A shower. What a treat for a pregnant woman, she had said to Paul.

"There aren't many streets like this in Minneapolis," the agent had told them. Wood-shingled homes converted into multifamily dwellings, lined up in a charming Victorian row. They had had one weekend to choose an apartment, and all the agent showed them were high-rise apartment houses. They had wanted an entire floor in a house. Amy had thought there might be mountains, but it wasn't true that the earth rose slowly and steadily till it came to the Rockies, then not quite so slowly descended again toward the Pacific Ocean. "What about Kansas?" Paul queried when she expressed her simplistic view of American topography. "'Rolling' is what we call it here," Doug Chambers had said to them. (Why did everyone think Minneapolis was so splendid?)

Doug and his wife Ellen were their Minnesota connection. You must look them up, Paul's father had said. Ellen was his second cousin once removed. You're nearly identical ages, you two, with Ellen and Doug, and blood ties have a way, you know, of transcending all other issues. What other issues were there? Amy had wondered. Were we to love them in spite of grotesque physical deformities? Intolerable and repulsive personalities? But Paul's father hadn't seen Ellen since she was a child and could give little concrete information about her. Doug was a graduate student in anthropology. Ellen was finishing her own degree in French, part-time. "We try to see a lot of theater in the summer," Doug said. "Winter evenings, you never know if you'll be able to go anywhere. It gets awful snowy here." Paul was not terribly keen on ice and tended to semihibernate in February. "A lot of ice?" Paul asked, but Doug said no, not like the East (he was from New England), just snow, and glorious amounts of it, so you could ski all winter and get around on cross-country skis. "You have skis, don't you?" Doug asked, and Paul said, just cross-country, but

Doug thought that was the most important. "I don't even own downhill," Ellen told them. Ellen had screamed — with pleasure, she was quick to reassure them — when she realized Amy was pregnant.

"If I'd known there were only apartment houses, I might not have been so anxious to come out here," Amy had said to the agent. Paul squeezed her hand gently.

"Now don't blame Mrs. Finster," he mediated gracefully. "It certainly isn't her fault we decided to move out here." A fun "explore," Paul had called this move. We can always move again if it doesn't work out, he'd said. "I don't suppose there are any flats in houses?" he asked.

"You prefer a wood structure?" she asked. "Not everyone does. Most people like the security of brick in multiple-dwelling units."

Then she drove them down a tree-lined street. The apartment she offered was too small. Perfect, Paul said, if it weren't that we were expecting a baby. The agent oohed and aahed. Was Mrs. Gold really pregnant, surely not very far along, could she be, looking so very tiny? (Oh come on, Amy thought.) Mrs. Finster pointed out the original, unpainted wooden moldings, the elaborately decorated brass doorknobs, the undersized but functioning fireplace. She suggested they sit on the window seat (bay window with charming little leaded glass) and just relax a bit, think about it, maybe. This was probably the only apartment that would come up on the street for a year. People just don't move around much in Minneapolis, she said. Paul said it was impossible. Amy said it was impossible, how could they manage with a baby with only one bedroom? "A baby only needs a crib," Mrs. Finster said. "That's all. It'll be years before you'll even need toy shelves." Her tone was sure, positively singing with truth. "I'd just string a sheet from here to here," she continued in her lilting way. She drew an imaginary line through the spacious passageway that separated living room from kitchen. "You must remember," she said, "that this was once the dining room. People used it as a room, not just as a place to walk through. You can reclaim it."

"We'd still have to walk through it," Amy said, "to get from one part of the apartment to another. We'd be walking through the baby's room. Waking him up all the time."

"It'll be divided," Mrs. Finster sang out. "Baby's room here," she said, indicating with a flourish the left side of the passageway, "hallway here," she said, showing them the small area in which they then stood. "A pretty designer sheet, of course," and here she raised both her arms as though preparing her audience for the finale in her series of tricks and illusions, and said, "Your baby'll have the most elegant abode in Minnesota."

"What the hell," said Paul, his finger tracing the pattern of a flower in the brass hinge of a door, "let's take it, Amy." The agent handed him a lease form.

"I hope you'll like us here," the agent said. "We're not real transient here, you know. Not much turnover. People either love us or hate us. You like snow?" she asked.

"We cross-country ski," Paul said.

"Well, that'll help," she said. "At least you've seen snow." She laughed. Amy wished she had brought a tape measure. It didn't look at all to her as if the area could ever have served as a dining room. Not unless the table had been long and narrow. "Woman on the third floor," Mrs. Finster explained as Paul took his checkbook out, "is eighty-nine." The agent's voice now rose in volume. Amy had begun to measure out the width of the area with her feet. She supposed Mrs. Finster hoped her loudness would prevent Paul from seeing what she was doing. "She's lived here for twenty-two years. Moved in when her husband died. Mrs. Martin. On the second floor, there's a young couple. Just married last year. Very nice. A quiet house. I hope you'll like us." The crib would fit, she thought, but just barely.

"Doug and Ellen like it here," Paul said as they'd settled into their motel for the evening. "They're from Boston, and they like it."

"Paul," she said, "maybe I should get a job. Maybe Doug can get us some information about private schools."

"I thought you were going to take time off for the pregnancy."

"I'm wondering now if that was the right decision."

"Who's going to hire you for a September job when you're already looking pregnant? It's not realistic."

"Afterwards," she said, "what will I say I've done after I stopped teaching?"

"Had a baby," he said. "That's what you will have done. You can develop a curriculum for private flute study. Then later, when you're ready, you can give lessons based on that." He pressed his palms along the surface of the mattress, judging its firmness.

"Not if I don't have some local references," she said. "I need a part-time connection with a prep school or something like that."

"By the time you're ready to start getting involved with the flute again, I'll probably know all sorts of people who can help you get going. You don't need a job now." He lay full-length on his back. "I think this bed's pretty good," he said.

But what would she do during the day? When there was a baby, that would be different. Then there'd be something to do. First thing, she'd have to find out when the other people in the house were out. Lots of people disliked the sound of solo flute. Especially when it was distorted through walls and floors.

The first time the telephone rang in their new home, it was the Welcome Wagon lady. Paul had answered the phone, climbing over cardboard boxes to do so, and said they weren't interested. "I should have just told her to drop dead," he said as he slammed the phone down.

"Was she insulting?" Amy asked. "Did she use foul language?"

"No," he said, he was just annoyed that the very first incoming call on his brand new (push-button) phone was from somebody trying to sell him something. Amy said she thought that a bit paranoid on his part since everyone knew the Welcome Wagon gave you free gifts and maps and service guides and other helpful things. "If you want to call them back," he said, "you can."

"It's not worth the embarrassment," she said. She was usually the nutty one, he the calm one. It was always his job to laugh her through her depressions. She wasn't sure she knew how to do the same for him. Maybe they had taken on too much at once. Everyone else seemed to think so. Even this small amount of irrationality in Paul disturbed her. She depended on him being in control, and craved, in her moments of confusion, his voice saying his familiar, "Now here's what we'll do . . . " But she knew she mustn't overreact: it was childish to think his little burst of temper was a symptom of complete dissatisfaction with their new life. Yet wasn't it, after all, her fault that they had come out here? They had been riding back from her mother's funeral, the days of mourning, the selling of her home and possessions. Right in the tunnel under West Rock she'd said, "Haven't we been in this town long enough?" The words had seemed to reverberate over and over inside the tunnel. Had she actually shouted them? Is that why they always sounded so loud in her ears when she recalled them? "Goddamn it, you're right," he had said. No more echoes, out of the tunnel. But he had said it over and over, "Goddamn it, you're right," and he continued to say it, all the way through dinner. They'd toasted their decision with each new variety of imported beer they'd ordered. It had seemed in bad taste to be laughing like that so close to her mother's death. "Should we put this decision off?" she asked him, and she noticed her own hands felt quite fluid after three beers. She wondered if she might take up dance again, as she watched her own hand gracefully pour Stohl's from bottle to stein.

"Do you mean, are you rational tonight?" She nodded. "Perhaps not," he said. "But perhaps you never are." They laughed together, and she filled his glass. He reached for her black hair and piled it in loose mounds atop her head. "You just be my geisha tonight, and I'll be rational for both of us tomorrow." He had grown silent then, let her hair back down, and said, quietly, "I think it's a good idea. I think it's time. Why do people always put things off? If we've learned anything from your mother's death, it's that life is short. If we want to move somewhere, we move, that's all. And if we don't like where we move, we move again." He could have vetoed the idea. In the tunnel. At dinner. The next day. Two weeks later. He hadn't. "The adventure begins," he had said the next day as he combed through the education section of the *New York Times* for administrative university positions. Too late now. We're in the land of summer, not winter, theater. She looked at him. He might pass for Scandinavian: dirty blonde hair, with a marvelously rough curly beard of blonde, red, and brown colorings. He was a large man, tall and substantial, yet not over-weight. She could quite easily imagine this man with the clearest of clear blue eyes as a swinger of axes in the north woods. Her own dark hair and dark eyes would give her away for what she was: a transient from the East Coast. And she was in good shape (not perhaps today, not with this belly attached across the front, but usually), but in very refined form — arms and legs of a dancer, hands of a flutist. Not Semitic, surely, not in the East, but out here? Here, she would appear Semitic.

Ought she to call the Welcome Wagon lady back and apologize for her husband? Ought she to explain it was all her, Amy's, fault that this whole silly situation had come about? "Do you hate me?" she asked him. He put down the large pile of books he held and reached for her hand. "Come here," he said, and as he sat down on the floor, he urged her onto his lap. "I love you," he said, and he held her and rocked her. "I love you, baby." He combed his fingers through her long black hair. "I promise I won't say any more bad words, OK?"

"OK," she said, and they had kissed.

Their second call came only a few moments later. "We'll see you tomorrow at two," she heard Paul say just before he hung up the phone. "Ellen and Doug," he told her. "They want to take us on a special tour of the Twin Cities." It would be good to begin to know the city, to begin to settle into it, she thought.

"But I've got to tell you," Paul said, "that she was going on and on about wanting to see how big you've gotten."

"Oh yech," Amy said. "Do we have to go? She's got some kind of fetish about pregnancy and she couldn't keep her hands off my belly last time. I think that's what your father must have been trying to warn us about. She's perverse, Paul."

"Why do you always have to be so judgmental?" he snapped at her. He pushed some cartons aside, pulled the last full one toward himself. "Can't you give anybody a chance?"

She had meant to be funny. When he's calmer, she thought, when he's back at the old nine-to-five in the provost's office, he'll be all right again. She watched him unpack the last of the dinner dishes. When we're back to normal, she thought.

Next day when the Chamberses came to pick them up, Ellen made Amy turn around so she could see if she was "carrying at all in the back." "Hasn't she popped since we last saw her?" Ellen asked Doug. He nodded and patted Amy's shoulder as he helped her into the car. Their Twin City orientation consisted primarily of discount houses and factory outlets. After all, Ellen said, what you really need to know when you get to a new city is the name of a good doctor and where to shop. Cheaply, Doug added. You don't want to get taken, just because you're a stranger. Later, off in the corner of a cut-rate glassware outlet, Paul whispered to her, "We'll do our own tour next weekend, and we'll have lunch somewhere that's sinfully elegant."

"They're silly, aren't they?" she whispered back.

"She's just your average lightweight," he said, and they laughed.

Monday Paul started work, and Amy walked around the apartment. In New Haven, they had always left for work together. They had returned home usually within an hour of each other. Their vacations had always come at the same time. After work on Friday, they had luxuriated in their mutual exhaustion, napped together, made love, then rolled out of bed for a restaurant dinner and a movie. Saturdays, they would clean their apartment and gather together dirty laundry for the laundromat. Saturday afternoons there was marketing.

As Paul got up from the breakfast table on his first official morning as an administrator at the University of Minnesota, Amy, still in a nightgown and robe, said, "Don't bother clearing things away." He laughed.

"I wasn't actually going to," he said. "I figured you needed something to do."

"Clearing breakfast dishes isn't likely to provide me with much direction for the day, you know."

"You don't have to do anything," he said.

"Should I get dressed?" she asked.

"Sure, if you feel like it." They kissed good-bye. She showered and dressed, made the bed, washed the dishes, gathered the laundry, and then sat down to make a shopping list. She walked to the local market and bought a chicken for dinner. After lunch she took a blanket out back and read till she fell asleep.

On Friday, Paul was exhausted. She had already napped, out back, with her book. He napped, and she lay next to him on the bed. After a half hour she asked him if they could go out a little earlier, maybe go to a Sears and look for an apartment-sized washer before they had dinner. On Saturday, they vacuumed and drove to the laundromat.

"If you could get some of this done, now that you're home," he said while they watched their clothes sloshing round inside the commercial-sized washer, "during the week, I mean, then we could have Saturdays for doing other things."

"Traditional marriage time?" she asked him. "Just all of a sudden, overnight?" She wondered if the air of the Midwest had affected him. "Peer pressure?" she asked. "What creep at work do I get to blame for making you see the failings of your wife?" The washer slowed, then stopped, and the brightly colored pile of clothes plopped to the bottom of the tub.

"It has nothing to do with anybody at work," Paul said as he pulled open the washer door and began to transfer wet clothing into a wire laundry cart. "And you don't have to if you don't want to. It's just a suggestion."

"You gain, I lose?"

"OK, I'm sorry. Forget it if you don't want to." He had wheeled the cart to the other side of the laundromat and was tossing clothes into the dryer.

"Marketing, too, I suppose?" she challenged and grabbed a bra he had tossed into the enormous drum.

"Amy, it doesn't matter."

"You know my underwear can't go in the dryer."

"I mean, whether you do this stuff or not. I wanted to have our Saturdays free, together. That's all." He reached in his pocket for change. "Do you have any quarters?" She didn't. He walked toward the attendant, a dollar bill already in his hand. She closed her eyes, waiting for the sound of quarters clicking into the coin slot. His hand was on her shoulder. "Listen," he said, "I'm sorry. I didn't mean to change us. I didn't mean to upset you. I wanted the best arrangement for both of us."

"It's OK," she said, covering his hand with hers. "I'm home, you're not. I just never was before. Having a baby changes the balance of power, I guess."

"You don't have to put it that way."

"The only real difference between our marriage and the marriages we've disdained was probably that they had children. That the woman was at home."

"Probably."

"You won't forget how to do the laundry?"

"I'm not really going to stop doing all these things. And when we get the washer at home, I can do it there, evenings."

"Will you forget how to cook?"

"I'm not a good cook."

"But you cook."

"What? Steak, broiled chicken, scrambled eggs?"

"And pancakes. You have to keep making pancakes. I don't even know how to make them."

"I will. You act like I'm metamorphosing into a different person."

"Maybe we both are," she said, and she held out her hands to him.

He accepted her hands, then folded them gently, like little square handkerchieves between his own two hands.

"Of course we're not. Anyway," he said, "some changes are for the good."

After a week, she knew the schedule of the people on the second floor. They didn't seem to rise until after Paul left the house. Then she heard them scrambling about, flushing the toilet, running the shower. She suspected they didn't eat breakfast, for there was little time between their alarm and the slamming of the outer door to the house. They let the alarm ring for several minutes, and although Amy could barely hear it through the ceiling, it made her uncomfortable to think of someone tolerating such a jarring noise over such a long period of time. While she drank her third cup of tea, she would hear them rushing down the stairs. They returned at five and were out every night but one by seven again. The evening they were in, they played their stereo loudly enough for Amy and Paul to identify orchestrated Beatle melodies. Paul groaned when he fully realized what he heard. "I'll die living under that," he said. "Don't they understand the sacrilege involved in adulterating that music?"

Amy laughed. "Such a purist," she chastized him. "We must forgive them because of their youth. Mrs. Finster says they're very young. And they're not here much." Several mornings Amy went to the front window to try to catch a glimpse of them, but she saw only their backs as they hurried down the street. From the mail, lying jumbled together in the front hall with her own, she was able to discern that their name was Henderson. It seemed foolish to ask them if they would mind the flute. They would never be there to hear it.

But there was still Mrs. Martin on the third floor to consider. Just before noon on the next Tuesday, Amy climbed the two flights of stairs to the third floor. She had gone only half a dozen steps when she found herself gasping to catch her breath. She stopped and waited till her breathing had eased. Was the baby competing with her for air? She stopped at each landing till she breathed normally, then knocked on the door of the third-floor apartment. There was no answer. The second time, realizing the woman might be deaf, she knocked harder. She heard someone walking toward the door.

"Yes?" a high-pitched voice came through the closed door.

"My name is Amy Gold, and I've just moved into the first-floor," Amy shouted through the heavy dark door. She wished she hadn't bothered. If the woman was deaf, it didn't much matter whether she played the flute or not, did it?

"Yes?" Had she not heard? Amy wondered, or was her 'yes' a signal to proceed?

"I've just moved in," Amy now shouted.

"It's not for rent," the voice told her through the door. Amy turned to go, but she heard the door open behind her.

"Hello," Amy said and extended her hand. "My name is Amy Gold. I live on the first floor now."

The woman opened the door wider. Her short hair stood in a soft puff of white all round her face. "My husband and I just moved in," Amy reiterated.

The woman took Amy's hand now. "Nice of you to come up, Mrs. Gold. I'm Mrs. Martin, won't you come in?"

"Oh, no," said Amy, "I don't want to bother you." Amy could see into the apartment now, and, dominated as it was by Victorian furniture and fabrics (including this wispy-looking woman's own dress), it had a dark, cluttered look. Mrs. Martin continued to hold Amy's hand, shaking it up and down with involuntary Parkinson-like motions.

"I'm having crackers and cheese," she said. "Please join me." Mrs. Martin turned and began to lead Amy by the hand. "I keep the shades drawn because of the heat," she told Amy. "Just that one, on the west side, I keep open, for a little light. Attic rooms are not desirable in the summer, although in winter, the heat does rise, they tell me. Then in the afternoon, I shut the west window, open the east. Move with the sun, you know." Amy sat where Mrs. Martin indicated, on a stool covered with floral crewel work, at a table with a fringed dark red table cloth on it. "My daughter-in-law does my shopping. Being on the third floor, I don't go out much. I make a list, and she brings it to me, but she's always getting cheeses I don't ask for. Do you like cheese? She's always trying to get me to learn their fancy names, too. Cheddar's my favorite, not at all fancy. I disappoint her, I know." Mrs. Martin cut a slice of cheese and passed it to Amy on a cracker. "Are you and your husband from around here?"

"We're from the East. Originally from Maryland." Mrs. Martin nodded.

"I had an uncle moved to New York. Never came back. I've been in this apartment more than twenty years. Didn't know when I rented it that it would be this hot in summer, although I should have guessed. Anyone with half a mind would know the attic was hot, but it didn't look like an attic, it looked like a house. And a nice small one, just what I wanted to pull round me after my husband died. I didn't need more. I never thought I'd live this long, either. Thought I'd be here a while, then pass away. Didn't think it mattered all that much what the place was like. If I'd known it would be so many years, I would have found something more gracious, I believe. Summer doesn't last long, of course, but it's hot with the shades up. So I keep them down. That's why it's so dark in here. I'll open them if you prefer."

"No," said Amy, "it's quite all right."

"I see you're expecting," Mrs. Martin said.

"Yes," said Amy.

"Not in the summer, I hope."

"Early winter." Mrs. Martin nodded approvingly.

"That's a good time. I had one baby born in July. Thirty-five hours of labor, and she died, that baby did, and I was sure it was because of the heat. I always thought, forever afterwards, that if it hadn't been so beastly hot that day, she might have lived. I think the cold air stimulates the lungs. You breathe deeper, you empty and fill your lungs more effectively, and I think if she'd been a winter baby, her lungs might have cleared. Couldn't clear in that damp heat." She passed Amy another cracker with cheese. "I hope I haven't rattled you," she said. Amy shook her head. "You shouldn't worry, not in these modern times."

"Do you have other children besides your son?"

"Just the one." The woman ran her hand distractedly through her puff of hair. "But I had others that died. All my girls died. They said my second died because she was so early. When they come early, they sicken, often. She was so early, and so thin, I knew with that one she wouldn't make it, even though she did live a day. First one died right off, in the hour, but the second, she lived a day. The first one I called Annabelle. Isn't that a lovely name? And I called the next Annabelle, too. None of the others were that tiny. The other girls were older when they died. I called the next Eveline. She was a lovely thing. All white blond hair." She ran her hand lightly over her own whitened curls. "Fine one day and dead the next. Meningitis. You couldn't do anything about it then. I had Michael by then, and I thought they might both go at once, but Michael was strong, right from the beginning. He never got sick that time. Then later there was Margaret. She was always frail. I knew I wouldn't be able to keep her. She'd cough, and I'd think, this is the end. Say good-bye to Margaret. She was four when she died. Flu. It's rare, now, for them to die like that. Not back then. No antibiotics, you know." Amy nodded.

"Now, you can plan things out. You can count on your children surviving, can't you?"

"Yes," Amy said.

"So," said Mrs. Martin, "how do you like it out here?"

"It's very nice," Amy said. "We had friends drive us around a few days ago. It's pretty. Downtown is nice."

"Oh yes," she said. "Downtown is nice. We have buildings now with gardens right inside them. Middle of winter you can go downtown and feel like it's springtime. And the lakes. We've hundreds of lakes, you know. In the winter, I don't get around as much anymore, but then at least there's sun coming through the windows." She handed Amy another piece of cheese, and her hand shook more violently than before. Mrs. Martin eyed her own disability. "I don't understand those hands shaking. I try to keep them steady, and they won't." Amy glanced down at her own smoothly tanned hands, moved her fingers slowly to form a fist and saw her blue veins rising, her tendons announcing their presence. Mrs. Martin held her left hand in her right, then her right in her left. She extended them both, fingers pointing downward, for Amy's examination. Viewed against her pale whiteness, the brown spots and blue lines appeared as garish decorative additions. "Doctor won't do a thing for me. And do you know, I can't even write anymore. My writing flies up all over the page. Oh, I was a letter writer, too. I can crochet, though; that I can do. Calms the shaking somehow. I'll tell my daughter-in-law to bring me some baby yarn, and I'll get busy on a blanket for you. Yellow's good. You can use yellow either way, although I do think if you get a sallow baby, it only makes them look all the more sallow to put them in yellow. But I'll make that now, and we'll wait, why don't we, see what you have, and then I can make better colors, I think."

"Thank you," Amy said.

"You can leave the baby with me, anytime," Mrs. Martin offered.

"Thank you," Amy repeated. She tried not to stare at the woman's shaking hands, but she noticed, suddenly, that they were still and that, instead, her head now bobbed.

"It's so silly, this growing old," Mrs. Martin said. "I got my hands to stop, did you see that? But my head started up." Amy smiled politely.

"Would you mind," Amy asked, "if I practiced the flute downstairs? Would it bother you?"

"Oh, heavens, no," Mrs. Martin said. "That won't bother me at all. My husband played the French horn. I thought it a very silly instrument, myself. It never seemed to have much melodic quality to it. But the flute plays the melodies. I'd like that. Perhaps sometimes you could bring it up here and let me really hear it."

"Of course," Amy said, then rose to leave.

"If I can tolerate the French horn," Mrs. Martin said, "I can tolerate the flute."

Amy excused herself, saying she needed to get to the market. Did Mrs. Martin need anything? No, she said, she was fine. "But don't hesitate to stop by anytime," Mrs. Martin said. "You probably don't like old women," she continued. "Nobody really does, do they?"

"Oh," said Amy, wondering how to proceed, "I don't think that's true." She wished she could weave an elegant word-pattern of praise for the elderly, an even exchange for the promised baby blanket, but articulation failed her. "Good-bye," she said, and left.

Going down the stairs was decidedly easier than climbing up had been. Her descent was slow, but she was able to breathe normally all the way down.

Before leaving New Haven, Amy had bought herself special silvercloth for polishing the flute. It had been almost three weeks, what with the moving, the packing and unpacking, since she had even held the flute in her hands. Now she polished it carefully, making it perfect before she brought it to her lips, letting it catch the sun and reflect it back in dancing patterns on the ceiling and walls. She ran through a scale, and her breath came hard and gasping. Three weeks was long, she knew, much too long, but something else was wrong. She tried again, this time running through three octaves, but she choked awkwardly just as she neared the end. Like the morning on the stairwell: short of breath. Again she tried, but again she failed. She was like her students, unable to sustain a phrase, even a short phrase, now, with any controlled shape. She took the flute apart, not even wiping it — she had barely blown it; how wet could it be? — and clicked it away in its royal-blue velvet bed.

"It's not impossible that you might see some improvement in this as the pregnancy continues," her new doctor told her. "You may experience some improved pulmonary capacity later on. Of course, it may be a strain on your system to push it at this point, so if it's not essential, you might consider letting the matter rest just the few more months you have left. It's not essential, is it?"

"No," Amy said. "Not essential."

Three weeks later she began to bleed. The doctor ordered her to bed and placed a ban on baths and sex. She didn't panic. "If I lose the baby," she said to Paul, "I might not want another one right away."

"Sssh," he said, looking pained and depressed.

"Maybe not for a few years." He brought her a tray with a deli sandwich, an eclair, and decaffeinated tea. "Maybe never," she whispered when he carried the tray away. After a series of tests, the doctor decided it was nothing serious. Just be careful, he said. "Does he mean we shouldn't have sex?" Paul asked.

Amy called him back. "You can have sex," the doctor clarified, "just be careful."

"Tentative sex," Paul called it. "Careful sex. Silly and decidedly less than satisfying sex."

"At least it's sibilant," Amy said.

"At least it's sex," he said.

In her ninth month, she stopped going to the downtown noon concerts. She stopped coming into town to meet Paul. Instead, she read, often in bed, through musical texts and scores. The snow had already begun. She worried that she might fall. She worried labor might begin, right there on the sidewalks of Minneapolis. She worried that her membranes would break in the middle of Dayton's baby department and that she would stand there over an ever-spreading puddle. At first, she decided she didn't care, that she would walk on out the front door, pretending it belonged to someone else, and hail a cab. But finally, she opted for two afghans and the living room couch instead. Paul brought her books from the used paperback store he passed on his way home. 'Quicky books' he called them: mysteries and comic tales. At four-thirty, she would walk to the local market then come back and make dinner. After dinner, she would crawl back under her afghans. One evening, Paul rubbed her enormous belly with baby powder. "Why does my belly button have to pop out like that?" she moaned to him. "Will it go back again?"

"I'm sure it will."

"You can see it right through my clothes," she said. "It looks disgusting."

"I like it," he said, and demonstrated his veracity by kissing her poked-out navel. "We're going to change the world," he had said that night.

"What do you mean?"

"With this baby," he said, "We're going to add a new creature to the world. A never-before creature. A new person." She pulled the afghan over her head. He laughed.

What have I done? she began to say to herself. She repeated the phrase silently, and the repetitions were nearly soothing.

Three

THURSDAY morning, she dressed for the Infancy Worker's visit. Infancy Worker — what exactly did that mean? she wondered. The woman had made the appointment with her when she was still in the hospital. At the time, she hadn't even figured out how to breast-feed effectively, and she hadn't been sure she would live through a whole day at home with a baby. So she had agreed. "We can offer you practical, useful information, and you can help us identify problems of new mothers." Be helpful, get helped. It seemed quite logical then. But now she was more suspicious. She'd already been sought out by a dozen different individuals who were going to help her or give her something for the new baby. In each case, she had felt exploited.

There had been offers of free baby food, free photographs, and free diaper service. The woman who had called from Rest-Easy had seemed charming. She had commiserated openly about the difficulties of infancy. She had three children herself and worked, she told Amy, only part-time at home, raising a little extra money on the telephone. Her praise for Rest-Easy's generosity was profound. She grew confidential, saying how Rest-Easy's products were really superior to Carter's, just not as well known, not as well advertised. By offering free bedding this way — for that was what they did offer, two nursery print sheets and matching crib bumpers (they did need those, Amy admitted to the woman) — they hoped to expand their local market. A representative would drop them off that evening, and they would be absolutely free. No additional purchases, no shipping and handling charges.

The representative arrived as they were clearing away dinner. Amy attempted to accept the package and send him out the door, but he had come with a movie screen and projector. He wanted to explain the different product lines his company handled, he said. Amy reminded herself, as the man threaded the film into place, that he had just handed them fifteen dollars' worth of merchandise. When the lights went out, Marissa became restless. In the dark, Amy lifted her shirt and indulged the baby in a little snack. The Rest-Easy Company, it quickly became apparent, dealt primarily, not in bedding, but in fire-alarm systems. The film opened with a quick mention of this, then sped directly to full-color pictures of homes burning (Real pictures? Amy wondered, real homes?) and children screaming. (Voice overs?) Shots of charred baby cribs and distorted, blackened baby toys. When an interview with a weeping mother who had lost two children in a fire began, Amy had to leave the room. She forgot to break the suction seal of the baby's little mouth and, instead, pulled her off the breast and dashed to the bedroom. The nipple hurt for two days afterwards. Marissa screamed in protest. Amy wept for the woman on the screen. In the distance, she heard the noise of the film wind down suddenly. Paul, she later learned, had pulled the plug. She heard him threaten to call the police.

The following morning, Paul carried the sheets and bumper pads to the garbage can next to the garage. Amy had thought that particular measure somewhat extreme, but Paul would not be swayed. Packages continued to arrive, unsolicited, from other companies. Paul threw them all in with the rotting kitchen garbage.

He had resisted the Infancy Worker, too. What was her background? Who was she working for? She had worked, Amy explained, right alongside the chief of pediatrics in the hospital. "That doesn't mean a thing," Paul said. "What's the purpose of this study? Who's sponsoring it, for Christ's sake? And why be exploited by all these people, anyway? They all want something." Amy had thought she might ask the woman if there were any exercises or games she could do with the baby. She didn't "play" at all with Marissa, but that was because she couldn't figure out how to begin. She knew she wasn't typical — she didn't coo and sing to the baby — and she had begun to feel self-conscious about that. Was Marissa being deprived of something important, or was that kind of noisemaking as silly as it seemed to her?

"She might tell me something helpful."

"What?"

"How to do all this," she had said, gesturing broadly toward the infant's part of the apartment. "How other people do it."

Paul had shrugged and left for work.

Amy chose to take the corduroy chair for the interview with Laurel, the Infancy Worker. Laurel sat opposite her on the love seat. "Would you describe Marissa as an easy baby or a difficult baby?" she asked. Laurel passed Amy an unlined three-by-five card, laminated in plastic. It contained a five-point scale, ranging from one — extremely easy — to five — extremely difficult. Three was "neither difficult nor easy."

"Two. Or three, I suppose. A typical baby, I guess. I meant to ask on the telephone," she then said without a pause, "are you doing this study for the hospital?"

"No, I think I mentioned that the data will become part of my dissertation. But the hospital allows me to make my contacts on the maternity wing."

"It doesn't really have anything to do with the pediatric department, then?"

"Not directly."

"Indirectly?"

"My data may help them. I certainly hope it will. I anticipate it will help them understand the problems of new mothers more and make them more receptive to those needs." Amy imagined Paul's angry response had he been able to hear her words.

"Would you rather not continue?"

"No, it's OK. We can continue."

"Are you sure? You seem upset."

"No, I'll continue."

"Sure?"

Amy nodded. Laurel settled back into the love seat. "So now, would you like to answer two or three to that last one?"

"Two. She's an easy baby."

"OK," Laurel said and recorded Amy's answer. "Would you say the addition of a baby to this household has been: one — not at all disruptive — to five — extremely disruptive." Laurel handed Amy another card.

"I guess two." It was noted. I'm fine, Amy had wanted to shout at the woman. Fine, fine, fine. We're all fine. You'll get no secrets from me for your purposes.

There were forty-two similar questions, followed by more open-ended questions. Laurel ran through them efficiently. "What would you say is the single most difficult thing about having an infant?"

"Loss of sleep," Amy told her.

"Of the following people," Laurel continued, "which was the most helpful in the first weeks of being a new mother: your mother or another relative, a friend or neighbor, a doctor or other health worker?"

"My mother is deceased."

"One of the others, then?"

Mrs. Martin? Amy wondered. Would she qualify? She had wound her way downstairs with the yellow blanket in her hands right after Amy had returned from the hospital. She had sat in silence watching the baby and had then said, "I think I'll make her a pink hat. She ought to be wearing a hat in this weather." Indoors? Amy had inquired, and the woman had assented with a decisive nod. Mrs. Martin had then stood up immediately, her eagerness to begin her project and to ward off infantile pneumonia all too apparent. Paul had helped her back to the third floor. After that, Amy carried the baby to the third floor for Mrs. Martin's occasional viewing. The hat was presented, and dutifully, Amy wrapped Marissa in it for her visits to its donor.

"Who else was on the list?" Amy asked. Laurel read it again.

"A friend, perhaps?"

Amy considered. "Continuing support, do you mean?"

"That's one way to look at it, although not necessarily concrete or physical assistance is meant here," Laurel said. "Emotional support is significant support and help."

"Maybe the doctor," Amy said, hoping this would be the last question. Unless you told the pediatrician's receptionist that your problem was urgent, it could take two days for him to return a call. Lately he had begun responding to her questions with, "I want you to start making some of these decisions yourself, you know." OK, so she would. So she wouldn't call him anymore. Laurel had noted her response and had begun to sift through the papers, seeming to reorder them.

"And last of all, a few questions on marital relations. Would you say your marital relations have returned to normal?"

"We get along just fine."

Laurel said nothing, but shifted her position on the couch. "Have you experienced any problems?"

"Just the ones we talked about earlier, the sleep, not being able to go where and when we want to. But we'll work it out, I'm sure." Amy stood up. "Was that the last question?" she asked.

"Yes," said Laurel, standing too now, extending her hand. "Thank you for your help."

"When will I get the results?"

"Well, this is just preliminary data. From this data, I design my actual study for the dissertation and then collect more data, analyze it, and write the dissertation. I'm afraid it will take a while." She laughed and slipped her stack of papers into a manila folder.

"I guess Marissa will be in nursery school before I hear."

"I'm afraid it won't help you much this time around, but for the next one, you'll have the benefit of all the data." The next one. Why did everyone expect there must be another child after Marissa? The mere mention of it revived the tight feeling of the stitches along the path of her episiotomy. Amy heard the baby begin her call. As she reached to open the door for Laurel, the doorbell sounded.

"Mailman," he said, as he held out the day's package. She took it from his hand. He touched his cap, turned and walked down the path. Damn her, Amy thought, staying so long. Damn her. She tossed the package to the living room floor.

Next morning at Marissa's nine o'clock feeding, Amy thought about cookie recipes. What were the ingredients? Flour, sugar? Lots had brown sugar, she supposed. The sorts of things people were always supposed to have in the house. When Paul left for work, she pulled out cookbooks and began searching through them. Why did so many of them require chilling overnight? And there were no chocolate chips in the house. No chocolate at all. Not even cocoa. Maybe sugar cookies. How difficult could they be? Or spice cookies, maybe? Those contained brown sugar. No good. And butter, even the sugar cookies called for butter. Would they work with margarine? She would have to decide whether to try or just give up. "A simple recipe children love to make with on-hand ingredients." Just what she needed.

And was it margarine, after all, that was to blame? she wondered forty minutes later, as she drew the tray from the oven. The yellow cookies had spread unevenly, merging in twos and threes all over the tray. The raggy edges were brown, almost blackened in places, but the centers of the cookies, as she now determined by touch, were mushy. She lifted the edge of one tentatively with a metal spatula. The moist cookie accordioned into itself. She lifted it high then flung it from the spatula into the sink. Children, she thought, can make them. She went into the bedroom and switched on the TV. Talk show. Psychologist? sociologist? gesturing broadly while he talks about modifying the behavior of children so that parents can cope more effectively. The women (are they all overweight?) in the audience nod approvingly as he talks. "Is the caller there?" Phil Donahue asks and pushes buttons back and forth across the phone. Phil switches to the studio audience. "Let's get a man's opinion," he says, and scans the room, then pops up and runs to the back, waving his enormous microphone threateningly. "I agree with the speaker," the (also overweight) man says, shifting uneasily. "Parents need to work together, to agree on things." The women around him nod again. Phil runs to the front. This time the caller is there. "I'm at the end of my rope," the crackly voice says. "I have this twenty-month old." "Yes," Phil says, helping her flow. "And yeah," she continues, "she's always dumpin' out the Cheerios box on the floor, and I can't handle it. I just can't."

Phil looks puzzled. The guest looks puzzled. "How did she get the box?" the guest asks.

"She opened the cabinet."

"It must be down too low," Phil says, clearly looking shocked.

"The upper cabinets are all filled," she moans into the telephone–TV wires. The guest laughs. The audience, inspired by his irreverence, laughs, too.

"Sometimes," says the guest, "we overlook simple solutions."

The nodding begins again. Amy gave them the click, and the bedroom was dark.

The baby shattered the quiet. Damn, Amy thought, it can't be time already. On her way through the kitchen, she paused in front of the cookie sheet, poking a finger at the center of a cookie and noting that it had firmed up considerably. She lifted it from the sheet and transferred it to a cooling rack. It didn't bend. I can break off the burned parts, she thought. Marissa still cried. The next cookie she lifted over her head with the spatula, to check if it were burned. Acceptable, she decided. She lifted the others to the rack. She would bake the rest of the batter later. The baby's cry, her wee little cry, had become edged with despair (anger? can she feel anger already?) and had to be answered.

Four

THEY hadn't known when they moved in that only the north side of the house had storm windows. It was better than nothing, Paul said. As the temperature dropped outside, the crystals of ice grew, encroaching on still more of the inner surface of the unprotected windows. Amy would check the ice level in her living room as one might glance at an outdoor thermometer, following the minute fluctuations in the temperature as registered by that scale. Fascinated and compelled, she would sit next to those windows, the cold air coming in along the sill, chilling her bottom, and she would trace the shape of the upper curve of the ice pattern. Sometimes smooth and gently rounded, sometimes jagged, the ice rose like abstractions of mountain ranges in the distance. It would not always be like this, she knew. Eventually it would melt. Slowly, over a period of weeks, it would come down from its height two-thirds of the way up the window and recede, then grow soft and wet, till it was only trickling condensation for several weeks. Finally, it would disappear. Still later, she would even open the windows. It wouldn't last forever. At six months, the doctor had told her, the baby would stop vomiting so much. That would be about when she would be opening the windows. Things would improve. She scraped a pathway into the layer of ice with her nail. Perhaps by evening, certainly by morning, new ice would have formed in the channel she had created. Not as thick as the ice over the rest of the window. Like the tactile maps that are built up in the mountainous areas and seem sunken in the valley regions. What were they called? Topological maps? Geographical? Physical? Why couldn't she remember that? They were always in earth colors, brown for the mountains, green for the valleys. Weren't the oceans varying shades of blues and greens? This map was white. Completely white. Was that the baby already? She checked her watch. He was usually there by twelve-thirty. Sometimes it was later. He might not come. She certainly couldn't rely on it. She walked through the kitchen, and the unfamiliar sight of cookies on a blue plate arrested her attention.

The plate had been her mother's. They — she and her sisters and their husbands, her aunts, her uncles, her cousins — had all gathered together in her mother's living room on the day of the funeral. "Nobody's arguing," Uncle Manny had said to Amy and her sisters. "Not like some families," he kept repeating. "Some, they fall apart, fight over things. Bickering." She remembered her sister Julia's children bouncing on the couch, Julia yelling at them to stop. She had drifted from room to room with her sisters, a crowd of relatives following behind, careful not to pass beyond the doorways, for they were observers in another's home; a group on tour in a historic reconstruction. In the end, no one took very much; trinkets here and there, memory pieces. The aunts had certain requests which the daughters allowed them ("I gave these spoons to her," Aunt Estelle said, "I might as well take them back, don't you think?"). For Amy, there had been the blue plate. Chinese in spirit, American (Syracuse) in origin. Her mother's (and her grandmother's before that) cookie server. "For the baby in the family," Aunt Estelle had said when she held it out to Amy.

"Don't you think it's right that the cookie platter should go to the baby?" she asked the assembled group. There was some laughter. She had considered stashing the plate under her shirt but went, instead, to the attic, found an old gift box with tissue, and wrapped the piece carefully in it. It was all she carried away from her mother's house that evening.

Ought she to leave the plate on the table now, sitting, waiting expectantly for him? Would it look casual, as though she always had a supply of cookies lying about, or would it look planned, manipulative even? If they were put away, in a tin — there might be one somewhere — there would be the obligatory polite protest as she went into the cabinet. "Please, don't go to any effort for me . . ." She didn't like protestations and explanations. She would leave them on the table. And there was milk. (Christ, she couldn't offer the man cookies and milk, could she, just because she was a nursing mother?) No, the offer would be for tea, the cookies would just be there. You couldn't invite someone in for tea and not serve anything.

He had come as early as eleven-thirty once, she remembered as she changed Marissa. Had he ever come later than one? Maybe. In the beginning, she hadn't noticed the time, hadn't realized it would always be him bringing the one or two new gifts for the baby. Where was he? Had she not heard him perhaps? Why had she ever been so foolish as to suggest that he knock? She paced with the baby in her arms. Marissa cried and strained and twisted toward Amy's breast. "All right, already," she said aloud, and strode toward the living room. Marissa gulped noisily at the breast. Amy stood, pulling her loose sweater down over the baby, then, with her free hand, opened the front door and peered into the hall. Mail, pushed through the slot, some for her and Paul, some for the tenants upstairs, lay scattered in a fanlike pattern across the floor. That wasn't his mail. His packages wouldn't make it through the slot. He might have left it outside the door. She opened the outer door and leaned out. No package. Marissa released the nipple as the cold hit her. Amy stared into the snowy path. Footsteps, but how many? It was impossible to tell. With snow day after day, the way it had been this week, with footsteps permanently freezing into the surface of the earth, she couldn't tell. He might have come. He might not have.

At two o'clock, she began to search for the tin. She had a sense, although they had lived in the apartment since August, that she was searching through someone else's cabinets. Of course she knew where her plates and glasses were, and the pots and pans, but the other things — the small appliances, the large platters, the strainers, ricers, and other equipment — looked strange to her. The tin itself, when she had located it, seemed foreign, too, its Currier and Ives cover entirely unfamiliar. How had it come to be in her kitchen? Had there once been a gift of cookies? Or fruit cake? She couldn't place it. She pulled lengths of aluminum foil to fit the bottom of the tin, then piled the cookies in. They were softer than they had been in the morning. Were they going to turn mushy again? Perhaps keeping them in the air had done that. She tossed them in haphazardly. They were supposed to be crisps, damn it. They were called lemon crisps, not lemon rags. Some of them stuck to one another. They felt damp now, as though the shortening were suddenly coming to the surface. The lousy margarine, she thought: substitutions are always a mistake.

Now, if she were to tell Paul about the cookies, it would seem odd, wouldn't it, cookies but no dinner. If she were to make dinner, however, the cookies would just be nice, an extra. She'd have done more than even he would have expected. Above and beyond the call of duty and all that. But there was still her own lunch. She could have toast. She would have to drink milk. Four glasses per day. But there was no point in eating when Marissa was asleep. She would lie down, otherwise she might not get another chance before it was time to prepare dinner. She went into the bedroom and turned on the silent TV picture. Not Mona now, but Serena. Brow-beaten, defeated. Sad Serena, sad Mona, she thought.

"Would you like some tea?" she asked him, and hearing no immediate response, she continued, "Is it allowed? To come in and get warm a bit, or will you get in trouble?"

He hesitated. "For a couple of minutes," he said, but he still held back. "I don't want to interfere, though. I mean, there's the baby. There's things you'll have to do."

"It's OK," she confirmed.

He stood in the hall, stamping the snow off his boots. "These boots," he said. "I'll need to slip them off." She nodded. She turned away toward the living room. Privacy for boots? There were shoes underneath: what on earth had she been thinking? She turned back to him. He had removed his outer jacket, revealing a heavy blue sweater underneath. Government issue, she supposed. His cap was gone. He wasn't grey.

"I'm Amy," she said as she took his outer clothing from him.

"I know," he said. "Mrs. Amy Gold. Mother of Marissa Gold."

"Yes," she said.

"Mrs. Paul Gold," he continued.

"Yes."

"OK," he said, rubbing his hands together and stepping into the living room. "And I'll bet anything your maiden name was Siegel, right?"

"Right."

"A lot of packages with that return name. Had to be your family, I figured. You're from Maryland, then?" She nodded. "Warmer there, I guess."

"Not all this continuous snow." She watched his feet shifting on the hall mat. She saw his weathered hand brushing the remaining snow from his pants legs.

"You'd better let me into the kitchen where I can't do any harm.

I don't want to drip on the floor." She turned toward the kitchen; he followed. "Where's the baby?" he asked from behind her.

"She's sleeping."

"Damn," he whispered, then added a hasty, "Sorry."

"Talking doesn't usually wake her," Amy assured him.

"Well, I'm not taking any chances," he continued in a whisper. "Mine didn't wake from talking either, but until they were a year each, I never talked full voice once, I think."

She filled the tea kettle. He sat now on one of the ice-cream parlor chairs. "We had chairs like this, once. Well, they weren't ours, I guess. We rented a furnished apartment the first year we were married. It had two chairs, just like this."

The tea kettle began to make little preboiling noises.

"How many children do you have?" she asked him.

"Five."

"Oh, my," she said. "I think I'll stop at one, myself."

"It only starts to really be fun when you have two," he said. "Then it's a family. We had ours close together in the beginning. Just a year apart. The first three. Then we thought that would be all, just three, but when the youngest was ready to go to kindergarten, we both got sad — no more babies and all — and decided to have another. And then, we figured we might as well have one more so there'd be two the same age. For companionship, you know, for each other."

She turned to look at him. Forty, but no more, she thought. He pushed his straight black hair off his forehead as she looked at him. About Paul's size. A little shorter, perhaps, and his face was smoother; no sign of a beard. A simple straight nose, regular sort of lips. A simpler face than Paul's. "Is your name Joe?" she asked him suddenly.

He laughed. "Eddie," he said. "Why'd you think it was Joe?"

"I made up a name for you," she said. "It was the first one that came to my head."

"Joe, Eddie. Whichever you like." They laughed together. "Infancy goes by so fast," he said, shaking his head. "I cried every time one of my kids advanced. Each tooth, I cried. When they walked, I cried. When they talked, I cried. When they went to nursery school. I love babies."

She turned back to the stove before he finished the speech. It was her fault, she supposed. She had raised the question of children. She had opened the topic for conversation. The bubbles in the glass tea kettle were beginning to crash into one another. She'd never noticed before how the gas hissed when something was cooking. It was really quite loud, and the whistle was gaining, growing, approaching a fine, thin screech.

"One of the kids," he said from behind her, "she used to come running in, no matter where she was in the house, and say, 'Tea, Daddy,' when she heard the kettle boil. It got so I couldn't hear a whistle without that little phrase, 'Tea, Daddy,' in my head. Like a reflex, I guess. You know, Pavlovian or something."

Funny, she thought, how the water changes, depending on how high or how low you hold the kettle when you pour it into the pot. Kind of splashy at certain heights, really.

"Don't burn yourself," he said. He stood then, reached for the sponge, and began wiping the pool of water that had formed around the pot. He carried the pot to the table, she managed the cups.

"Are you all right?" he asked after he had poured them each a cup of tea.

"Yes."

"There's a lot to do when you first have a baby." His statement hung lightly in the air, waiting for a breeze, a tiny waft of warm air, to turn it into a gentle question.

"Yes," she said, and she watched the pattern of her fingers interlocked around her teacup.

"It does get easier," he said, and that statement turned and spun near her teacup, almost, but not quite, metamorphosing into a joke. When it faded, his smile, which had momentarily looked as though it might become a laugh, faded also.

"What's the worst?" he asked.

"Loss of sleep," she said woodenly. He nodded.

"Tell me where the sugar is," he said. "I just need a touch for my tea. I'm a bit of a baby about that."

"I'm sorry," she said, standing.

"Sit down," he said. "The mother needs to be cared for just as the baby does." He put a hand on her shoulder. "Really," he said, "just let me do one or two things for you." She pointed to a cabinet. "Anyway," he said, as he drew out the sugar bowl, "I'm the one who wants sugar, not you." He sat back down. "Every time that baby goes to sleep, you should sit down and put your feet up." He glanced about. "Good thing there's three chairs, isn't it?" He laughed, and she liked the laugh — a smooth, even, controlled laugh. He positioned the extra chair opposite her own. "Now," he said, "just put your feet up here, come on." She did so. "You're in need of care," he said. "New mothers should have their feet up as much as possible. Is there more tea in there?" he asked, indicating the teapot. "Don't move," he said, as she began to lean toward the table. He poured for both of them again. He sat back in his chair, too, his own legs stretched out on the floor in front of him. "I can't say I mind this break," he said. "These winters seem to get colder and colder, don't they?" He looked away. "I'm going to have to keep an eye on you. Make sure you really take care of yourself."

"I think I need care," she whispered. Amy heard Marissa stirring. Spoiling things again. He had heard her, too, and rose from his chair.

"Can I just see her before I go?" he asked.

"You don't have to go," she said.

"I ought to," he said. "Besides, you need to feed her."

They walked into the alcove where Marissa lived. Amy lifted the baby from the crib, then held her, her face contorted in a cry, for him to view. "My God," he said, "what a miracle she is. A delicate little beauty." He looked intently at Amy. "She looks like you," he said. "Is that what everyone says?"

"Mostly."

"All right, I'm taking off now. You take care of her, and I'll find my way out." He put his hand on her arm. "You take care of yourself, too. I'll see you in a day or so, I'm sure."

She followed him to the door. Marissa had begun to cry. Amy felt the fierce sting of the milk in her nipples. "I had baked you cookies the other day," she said. "The day you skipped. They weren't very good, really. They got all mushy."

"You're an angel," he said. "I'm sorry I missed them, but don't you dare make any more cookies, you understand? You're supposed to conserve energy, not waste it on me, OK?" She nodded. She watched him pull on boots, heavy jacket, and watch cap. He lifted his Post Office hat in salute to her, then settled it on top of his woolen one. "I'll be back," he said.

"I'll be right here," she told him.

Five

HE stopped for tea with every package, now. She could not, of course, tell Paul. She had to be careful what she said, but it wasn't difficult. It was almost fun. The matter of the spaghetti sauce was especially interesting. Amy felt herself flush with energy as she described "Adventures in Italian Home Cooking," the supposed source of her new recipe. It's so easy to make things up, she thought. Details for the tale came to her faster than she could make use of them. "A real emphasis on hearty cuisine. Peasant-style cooking."

"What was the chef like? A Julia Child type?" Paul inquired with interest.

"Not just one chef," she ad-libbed admirably. "Different chefs and recipes for the different regions — or at least," she quickly added when he looked ready to probe more — "I think that was what it was. I had to jump up and get Marissa and nurse her. It's hard to concentrate with a baby nibbling at you. But I did get this recipe down accurately." She showed him the recipe, taken down from Eddie's dictation the day before. "Afternoon TV's not so bad, is it?" she teased.

"It's not TV in itself that bothers me," he began, and she was glad she had the thin spaghetti to watch as it wrapped itself round her twirling fork. "It's those soap operas. You're too smart for that, that's all." A lovely spaghetti sauce, she thought.

"I like this thin spaghetti," he said. "Let's get this kind from now on."

A nice conversation, she thought. It really was.

She watched Paul across the table. He was glorying in his spaghetti, practically kissing the fragrant rich sauce every time he brought it to his lips. She laughed out loud, now, and he smiled back at her, as she thought of their degenerate eating binges of long ago. Early in their marriage, much of their salaries had gone to day after day of restaurant eating: French country for lunch, Indian for dinner, Vietnamese for lunch, and Japanese for dinner. Finally, they would be sated. They would return to their apartment and moan and groan over their distended abdomens, eat the straight and narrow for a week or two, and then, gradually, one of them would start saying, in a whisper, late in the afternoon, early in the evening, words like "crown roast," or "crispy duckling," or "Black Forest Cake," and soon they'd be off again, oohing and aahing over that preparation or this, switching forkfuls back and forth across the table, and laughing happily together.

What would Paul say if he knew the real source of the recipe? Would he stand and roar the words, "the mailman?!" at her, his ochre mustache bristling visibly? If this were the soapies, he might even tie her up when he left the house, or lock her in from the outside, although with that ice, she was little better than locked in, anyway.

No matter how simple, how innocent, this real situation was, if informed, Paul would be uncomfortable with it. Because the visitor, the giver of the recipe, was a man. Because he wasn't Ellen, because he wasn't her roommate in the hospital or some big fat blubbery woman who ate chocolates but who lived down the street and happened to have a two-month-old, too. And every night at dinner he'd look across at her, not at the food, as he did now, admiring it, thinking she was doing well, but wondering what she did with the mailman, creating sordid scenarios for her, phrasing, all the way home in the snow, what he would ask her, till finally, "How'd your day go?" would become "So what'd you and your mailman do?" or "D'you play post office again today?"

And it wouldn't be his fault, Paul's fault. She was in a situation that was perfect for the stand-up comic. Perfect domestic fight material, divorce material. Not because she was unfaithful, but because the imagery was ludicrous: he was a mailman, she a frazzled mother.

How much better to keep it a secret. Was it so terrible for the short time the packages would continue to come to let him help? Tonight there was a sense of magic in the air over dinner. Paul admired her skill tonight. I want to be good at this, she thought, and Eddie can help me, but only if I don't tell.

At first Amy hadn't let Eddie make the spaghetti sauce for her.

"I make it for my wife," he had said. "Once a week I put up a pot of sauce before I go to work. It's great sauce, Ame, and it's real easy. I'll give you the recipe," he had said as he poured them each a cup of tea. "You can make a double or triple quantity and freeze some of it."

"I'd like the recipe," she said but had suddenly been unable to look at him again.

"And if I have a package tomorrow, I'll cook it up for you. Demonstrate the technique and all, OK?" She still looked away. "Amy," he said, lightly touching her fingers as they entwined about her cup, "you really learn it that way. What do you think?"

"OK," she said, "we'll make it together."

Eddie called the neighborhood grocery store and ordered the ingredients. "Don't tip him too much," Eddie said. "Fifty cents is plenty. I always figure, if they don't like it, they don't have to deliver next time."

When the delivery boy arrived, long after Eddie had left, he explained, "Your husband wanted Progresso, but we was out of the paste. Delmonte OK?"

"It's fine," she said, and wished Eddie had been there to hear. She paid him, he made change, and then she handed him back two quarters. He had been polite. Thanked her. It had been the right tip. How easy it had turned out to be! She wondered why she had never thought of investigating home delivery before. There would be other things she could get taken care of that way. Department stores delivered. Fish stores delivered. She flipped through the yellow pages, underlining "we deliver" and "no charge for delivery" with a red marker wherever it occurred. "There's hamburgers and salad for dinner," she told Paul the moment he walked in the door. Eddie had suggested she order an extra pound of meat when she placed the order. There would be hamburgers one night, served with half the salad ingredients she had ordered. Spaghetti and meatballs the next night, with the other half of the salad.

"Things are looking up," Paul said as he shook the snow from his coat. Amy had to agree. It did look as though things were getting better.

Eddie became punctual. He still did not come every day, but when he did appear, package in hand, it was always close to noon. The grocer kept her well supplied now. Cold cuts, cheese, V-8 juice for him. Sometimes Eddie would bring fresh Italian bread. The snow ended, but the temperature dropped and stayed down. The winds came up, and the news advised that the elderly and very young be kept indoors. The grocery would not deliver for two days. Paul and Amy went back to eggs. But it wasn't her fault. Amy could no longer see out the front windows. She scraped the ice off the top third of one window each morning, but twenty minutes, maybe half an hour, later, the ice had grown back. She dragged a floor lamp to the window and shone it directly on the glass. She could control it that way. It wouldn't melt the thick part, but it would keep it from regrowing where she had scraped it. After Eddie left, she would turn off the light.

One time, the baby wakened just as Eddie walked in the door. "Sounds very hungry today, doesn't she?" he said. "I'm going to go." He started to rebutton his jacket.

"Why?"

"So you can feed her. You can't put them off when they're that hungry."

"You can stay," she said. Amy pulled a rocking chair away from the wall and adjusted the cushion on its seat.

"You use the rocker?" he asked. She nodded. "I'll wait in the kitchen," he said.

"You can wait here," she said, indicating the couch.

"Maybe I should just leave today, Ame."

"Why?" she asked him.

"The . . ." He put his hand to his chest, then gestured toward her. With eyes averted toward the baby in her carriage, he quietly said, "The breast-feeding."

She glanced at the ice. It was so cold, no children had tracked through the yards after the last snow. There was pure white snow all around the house. Except for the walk, of course. The Eskimos actually lived in the snow, in cold weather like this, didn't they? Lay about on animal skins inside their huts and igloos. She could wrap Marissa in a piece of fur and lay her down on the snow. It might be pretty. A little baby — and Marissa's hair was getting quite dark now — the contrast would be effective against the snow.

"OK?" he asked.

"What?"

"That I go today."

"Why don't you wait in the kitchen?" she asked, as she lifted the baby from her nest. Eskimos must have nursed their babies in front of one another. Where else could they go? Or did igloos come in two- and three-room versions? she wondered and held Marissa tightly against her. When summer came, she thought, rocking now in the chair, she would have a baby party. She would invite everyone she knew with babies. There was the woman who had shared her room at the hospital. And there had been two nice couples in the childbirth class. She would try to remember their names. Perhaps they hadn't even had their babies yet. They would sit on blankets in the backyard, and when the babies cried, they would nurse them. No one would mind. They would wear white gauze dresses. The kind that were gathered or elasticized at the top so you could just pull them down for a feeding. They wouldn't have to wear white, of course, but that would look pretty in the yard. And maybe there would be flowers. Or maybe the dresses would be embroidered. And they could feed their babies. No one would mind.

"I'll see you tomorrow," he said, as he finished lacing his boots.

When he was out the door, she lifted her shirt and Marissa dove for the nipple. Amy curled down into the chair and pulled her knees up around the baby. "Just you and me," she said, as she poked at the damp circles her tears left in the baby's thin hair. She cupped her hand round the baby's tiny head. The warmth was intense. Hair like silk. The baby's small hand shot up suddenly in a strange and random gesture. Amy reached for it, and the baby's tiny fist opened and closed round her pinky. "Talk to me," she whispered. "Please."

Thursday there was no package. Friday there was no package. Then there was the weekend. On Monday Ellen called and asked about the baby. They hadn't bothered since Friday's storm, Ellen said, to dig out the driveway. She had wanted, she said, to pick up groceries for Amy if she needed them, but didn't think the plow would be there till afternoon. "I'll die if this weather doesn't ease up," she told Amy. "I can't stay in anymore. I just can't."

"It's all right," Amy said. "I phone-order now."

Amy went back to the front window and sat, waiting. She pulled her fat sweater round her, tucking it, as well as she could, beneath her. When the baby awoke, she changed her as quickly as possible, turned up the thermostat, and returned to the front of the house to feed her by the window. At twelve-thirty she placed the baby in the carriage, then pushed it back and forth across the short length of the living room. From time to time she peered through the front window, stamped her feet in rage, and began her carriage pushing anew. At twelve-forty the truck pulled up. She opened the door before he got to the steps.

"Two things. Your package," he said as he handed it over, "and a special treat. It's why I'm late." He handed her a brown paper bag. She put the package down and reached into the bag. Linzertorte cookies. Raspberry jam, powdered sugar. She remembered her grandmother striding up the front steps Sunday afternoons, a box of cupcakes in one hand and a box of linzer tortes in the other. The cookies were thick and gently scalloped all around, just as they had been then. "I like these," she said.

"Good," he said as he pulled off a boot. "There's a wonderful bakery in Milton. It's out of the way, but it's worth it."

"Thank you, Eddie." The baby whined.

"Is she supposed to sleep now?" he whispered.

"Yes."

"Can I pick her up? Rock her to sleep, maybe?"

Paul was very firm about not picking Marissa up when she was supposed to be sleeping. "Why give her positive feedback for negative behavior?" he had said.

Eddie leaned over the carriage, then turned back to Amy. "Would you rather I left her alone?" She needn't tell Paul, of course, but he might be right about the spoiling.

"After a while," Eddie said, "when they're two or three, they can't be bothered with hugs and kisses. This age, though, you can steal a few kisses, and they don't even know." He rocked the carriage gently by its handle. She motioned toward the carriage, indicating her consent. Eddie scooped the baby into his arms. "Hello little baby," he said and nuzzled his nose against her cheek. "I'll get her to sleep in no time."

It would be nice, she thought, not to have the presleep crying for once.

He held her. Even after she slept. He held her the whole time they drank their tea and ate their linzer tortes. He made Amy put her feet up again. When he left, he lowered Marissa slowly into the carriage. She didn't wake.

After he left, she couldn't get Eskimos out of her head. She examined the windows for diversion. The windows had changed. Instead of the steeply formed mountains of ice with narrow cedar-like ice trees growing from them, there were feathery-looking patterns today. Eddie said it was because the temperature had gone up. He said it was expected to go as high as twenty-five degrees and that it felt like spring. The feathers were prettier than the trees. Softer. There were some spaces between them on one of the windows and she could see across the street to the peaked roof of the old grey house, where a bird convention seemed to be taking place. Fat, self-satisfied little puff-bellied birds were lined up in the snow. The snow had slid down the peaked roof, exposing some of the grey shingles, but the birds had chosen the snow, not the cleared portion. Some began to bounce about in the snow as though it were water and the roof was their bird bath. Fat. Puffy. Puff birds. They would have some other name. Grey warblings, perhaps, or white-winged roof nesters. Something. Like little fat Eskimos snuggling down in the snow. "I feel toasty warm even with the heat turned way down," the TV actress said, and the camera focused on her getting into bed next to a handsome young man. Amy walked closer to the TV and stared intently at the man. She was quite sure it was Etan. "I hope poor Mona's not watching TV," she said aloud and laughed. Eskimos might make good use of flannel sheets from Linder's, but Linder's didn't have a mail-order catalogue as far as she knew. Furs were probably warmer, weren't they? But were Eskimos ever really able to take off their clothes? Or did they just pile fur after fur upon themselves from October to April, maybe stripping off one of half a dozen or so layers around March. Wouldn't they roll about if they tried to lie down? Hadn't she read somewhere that Eskimos had special openings in their clothing so they could make love in the winter without stripping? Perhaps she had made that up. When you lived in that climate, you grew accustomed to the cold. You were able to remove your clothing and survive. But wouldn't skin stick to the ice? Eddie said it felt like spring. At twenty degrees. People adapted. Or perhaps they only made love in the summer. Surely, that was more likely.

Six

"IN my other life," she painstakingly wrote, "I was a flutist."
Amy held up the paper and examined it. She liked the way it
looked. It looked very nice. She would send it to someone. Not
like this, of course, not written on a sheet of yellow legal paper
with a blue Bic pen, but on Crane's, perhaps. Ecru Crane's. She
had some in her desk. Or was it her closet? She opened the desk
drawers one at a time and pulled the contents out. Why was it she
felt, as in the kitchen, that these were someone else's drawers?
Whose things were these? "Paul's," she said, just audibly. A pile
of photographs slid out of an envelope onto the desk. Black and
whites of his family. A picture of her mother and father, arms
linked, lay on top. Her mother. Her father. Smiling. Hugging.
When had they looked like that? He with hair, she with round girl
cheeks. Before children they might have looked like that. It wasn't
marriage that changed people and changed relationships, it was
children. It was only common numerical sense, after all. Before
there was only one person you had to love, and then suddenly two,
or three, or four. You had to take that same amount of love and

divide it up into smaller and smaller pieces for distribution throughout the whole family. She lifted the envelope and pushed all the photos back inside. Pushed all the papers, folders, maps, calendars, and bankbooks back into the drawers.

First, she would deal with the pen. She would need a fountain pen. Not calligraphy, for that would be too flashy, too silly. How might she get a fountain pen delivered? Were drugstores likely to carry them? She pulled the sheet of legal paper from the pad, placed it carefully to one side, and began to write anew. "Disposable diapers," she wrote. "Baby vitamins." She stopped. Couldn't she make it look more important? Wouldn't they plead only emergency deliveries in this weather? "Aspirin," she wrote. That might give it the look of influenza. Beneath that she wrote "baby aspirin," "baby Tylenol," and "baby nose syringe." That looked more compelling. You only needed a nose syringe if a baby were having difficulty breathing. That would get a delivery, she was certain. "Fountain pen, black ink," she wrote. She underlined the *black* several times. "Small spiral notebook," she added. Perhaps, if she couldn't find the Crane's, she would enter it in a notebook. Dated. She could save it that way till she found the Crane's. She read the list again. "Baby thermometer" she added at the bottom. In that context, the fountain pen and notebook might look necessary for keeping a record of the baby's temperature. An obsessive doctor might have ordered that, especially for a very ill baby. Now she was certain they would deliver.

When she had called in the order, she tiptoed to Marissa's crib. The baby slept quietly, peacefully. She had heard of babies, fine healthy babies who had simply died during their naps. Sudden-infant-death syndrome. Or babies with little colds who had gone to sleep and slept themselves into dehydration. Nearly fatal (maybe fatal?) dehydration. Fine one day and dead the next, Mrs. Martin had said. Perhaps it had been a sixth sense she had had in ordering all the baby medication. What if she were ill now? Amy reached in and lifted the baby up. Marissa whined, struck her fist out toward Amy, then closed her eyes again. Amy kissed her forehead. How was she to tell? How would she know? If they die without warning, how can you prevent it?

Eddie was adamant about not taking the baby's temperature. "She's cool," he said and continued slicing bread.

"I'm afraid to do it myself," she said. "She's so little."

"You're afraid because you know it's ridiculous. If she was sick, you'd just do it. There's nothing wrong with that baby. She's healthy."

"Some of them die," she said, "without warning."

"Yes," he said. "And it's very sad, but you can't prevent it, no matter what you do. If there's no warning, there wouldn't be a fever, anyway. You can't perch on the edge of her crib, eyes wide open, twenty-four hours a day, can you?"

"No."

"It won't help to worry." He made the tea. He cut slices of French bread; spread butter, sugar, and cinnamon on it; then watched through the glass door of the toaster oven till the surface bubbled. "It won't happen. It won't." He passed her two pieces of toast on a plate. "Concentrate on something practical. Write thank-you notes or something." She would have to look for the Crane's after all. "They all grow up, Ame, they all do. You wonder how, but they all do. Wait till you have two. You'll wonder how it is the first doesn't kill the second every time they go into a hug. The older one always seems to get the younger one round the neck. Hammer locks." He put his hand on her shoulder. "Do you like my toast?"

"I do," she said.

When he had gone, she opened her new notebook to the first page, uncapped the pen, and tested it carefully on the legal paper. The ink flowed smoothly. The point was fine and clear. She would have to learn to write without pressure, skimming the surface of the paper. She tried her sentence again on the legal paper: "In my other life, I was a flutist." Then slowly, she copied it into the notebook. She waved her hand over it, drying it thoroughly. At the top of the page, she placed the date. She had thought she would write more, but there seemed nothing else to say. She turned a page. "Sometimes," she wrote, "babies die for no reason." She recapped the pen, ripped the page from the notebook and crumbled it into a ball. She sat thinking a moment, then got a ruler from her drawer and walked to the window. When she returned to the desk, she wrote the date on a fresh page, and, under that, she wrote, "The height of the ice at its highest point is eighteen inches, the full height of the window. At its lowest point, it is thirteen inches." She closed the notebook, clipped her pen on it, then slid it beneath the jumble of papers in the desk.

At dawn the warm air mass, as predicted, moved in with precipitation. The mercury climbed to thirty degrees, and the ice on the window dropped two inches. Amy was asleep and could not note the change. The next day a hard thick layer of ice was added to every surface. Children, exultant at the still warmish air (it only dropped to twenty-seven degrees), slid about all over the neighborhood, the smaller ones walking blissfully on the surface of the ice-encrusted mounds of snow. By noon they had broken through all the surfaces, their little bodies falling into holes as deep as they were tall, and Amy's backyard was empty again. But they had left their mark. The snow had been broken up into huge, misshapen and asymmetrical blocks, scattered about at curious angles to one another. The front yard, the neighbor's yard, the entire world around her looked like the surface of an alien planet, forbidding and empty, but all white. No one, except a child masquerading as an explorer of the moon, would have dared to walk across it. The path to the front door, slick beyond imagining, had received some of the slabs that had slid off the huge mounds on the lawn. She watched Eddie negotiate the path. He sprinkled rock salt ahead of him as he walked. He thought of everything.

At night, she would lie awake, very very still, thinking in the dark. What if she needed Eddie? How would she contact him? She had never asked him his last name. He had never offered that information. She could make a joke of it now, laugh through the awkwardness of finally asking him, and he would probably tell her. Unless he liked it this way. He would stop coming when the packages stopped. If she were braver, stronger, smarter — something — she would be able to make him stay, long past the packages. When they had tea, she could reach for his hand, make it clear, do something. Say to him, you won't stop coming, will you? She repeated the question over and over in her head. She had to ask him.

"When do you bathe her?" Eddie asked.

"First thing in the morning," she said. She had read somewhere that that was an ideal time for a baby's bath.

"Our house is kind of cool first thing in the morning. Isn't this place?"

"I guess so," she said. She covered her cheeks with her hands, afraid he would see their color mounting as he questioned her. She washed the baby at no special time. And then it was only washing, not really ever bathing. A wet washcloth was surely enough, she had repeatedly assured herself. Marissa had hated the one bath she and Paul had tried to give her. Paul had said it couldn't be worth it. They could get her just as clean with a washcloth. And they — well, it had been Amy, Paul had watched — had almost dropped her. She was slippery. The baby had screeched the entire time, and long after the bath was over. She never wanted to do it again.

"They have those inflatable tubs now. You have one of those?" he asked.

"No."

"God, I used to love to bathe them. You wouldn't, sometime, want to give her a bath at noon, would you?"

"Maybe," she said and began clearing teacups from the table.

"You look like you're trying to get rid of me today." He laughed. "I didn't really want to finish my tea, anyway." He stood up.

"I'm sorry," she said, returning his cup to him and sitting again. "I was distracted."

"Are you upset?" he asked and pulled his chair nearer to hers. "Tell me," he said as he reached for her hand and held it between his own. The packages will stop, she thought. Next week two, the next week one, and then none.

"Tomorrow," she said, "will you come and watch the bath?"

"Of course," he said.

"What if there's no package?"

"Well, I shouldn't. When you're not on the route, I sometimes don't really end up down here at all."

"Even if there's no package," she said as she drew her hand away.

"OK," he said and took her hand back. "Tomorrow." They turned their faces simultaneously from one another. "I think I'll get going now," he said.

She watched him pull on his boots. "Eddie . . . ," she said, and she could hear the empty space after his first name. He looked up at her. "Joe," she began again as he started to reach for the door. "I don't know how to bathe her."

He walked back to her and put both hands on her shoulders.

"I'll show you tomorrow," he said and kissed her on the cheek.

When he was gone, she went into the other room and searched for her notebook in the drawer. She reread the first two entries, smoothing the words gently after she had done so. She turned to the third page and wrote the date, then stopped. "Bath," she wrote. Tomorrow she would write more.

If you finished your route and got all your packages delivered, Eddie thought, nobody really had anything to complain about, did they? Guys stopped off here and there. Some even had their families on their routes, stopped off and had lunch. Some had friends, whatever.

And poor lost thing, trying to be the gracious hostess. She just needed somebody to show her how to do things, so she could realize, hey, this isn't so hard, even though I've never done it before. There's a few little tricks you need to learn, and you need somebody to teach them to you, but that's all it is. People aren't born knowing how to diaper babies and all that, are they? Somebody has to show you that. He'd made the hospital nurse show him and Deena how to diaper that very first morning. He remembered how skinny Elizabeth was, no tone at all to her, either, and how he'd been worried that there was something wrong. And, of course, the doctors don't really have time for you. He always felt like he was getting patted on the head by them but never really told anything. But by the time Erica was born, he knew that was how they were supposed to look, so it was easier.

What worried him about Amy was that she held the baby so stiff. That didn't seem quite normal. She looked the way people do who've never held babies, who get handed one all of a sudden and don't know quite what to do, feeling all self-conscious, maybe, but worried, too, about dropping it or not holding the right places or something. At two months she should be easier with it. He tried to act real casual about it, even made that joke about how they're just like little puppy dogs, you've got to really play with them, pet them and all, so she would maybe see it wasn't so different from that, because everybody feels comfortable with puppies. She'd smiled a little, but still, she always looked glad to hand her over, poor thing. How he liked to take her, too. Maybe he shouldn't be so eager about it, though, for those very reasons. He ought to have her try to get more comfortable. He wasn't the one who needed baby experience.

All he had to do was feel that soft little head, smell that nice little baby smell, and he was hooked. How was she able to resist? he wondered. Deena had once asked him, would you have adopted if we hadn't been able to have kids, and he'd said, of course, but she said she wouldn't, she didn't think she could love someone else's child. Said she'd always be thinking of what kind of parents it had, and whether it misbehaved because it had lousy parents who were half-wits or irresponsible creeps of some sort, and that she'd reject it. But every time he held a baby, he felt the same. Anybody's baby. He wanted to kiss it and hold it and teach it everything he knew. And those unhappy kids that no one wanted — how easy it would be to take them and make them happy. When they're little, they're content with the barest essentials. In the beginning you keep them dry and fed. Then later you can make them happy with any old piece of garbage: ticket stubs from the movies, coupons from a magazine, empty boxes, or those stamps that come free in the mail from the record companies. They smile and laugh and go off and make up games. Now that his kids were older, they wanted this or that specific record or shirt or stuffed animal. Certain colors, or they were disappointed. It was work keeping them pleased. He missed the times when he could make them giggle just by the tone of his voice or the way he opened his hand to show them the silly thing he had for them. He'd been a magician then, pulling rabbits from hats.

He'd said to Deena, after the last one was in school, we could adopt now, and she'd said no, she didn't know how they could afford it, and maybe she was right. There was enough to go round now, but as they got bigger, everything was just going to get more and more expensive. He always seemed to have three kids taking ballet lessons — one would get too old for them just as another would be old enough.

Marissa, too, soon enough would be buying blue leotards and pink tights. Christ, it goes fast, he thought. She'll be dancing so soon.

Anyway, nobody really bothered you if you stopped off someplace. There'd been that old woman once, he'd taken the garbage out for. A couple of minutes now and then, if he could help somebody, was all right.

So what would he tell Deena? Simple and straightforward, he told himself. There's this new mother who doesn't know what the hell she's doing, so I've been helping her. Giving her advice. You know what I mean, I hold the baby for a few minutes while she puts a load of wash in. But it sounded so involved when he tried to put it into words. Why was he there when she was trying to do her wash; besides he'd just made that up, he'd never seen her do her wash. So what was it he did do? He had a cup of tea, and they talked about how hard it was to have a baby, and she asked him for advice (like what?) about things like when to bathe them and how to get them to stop crying when you bathed them, and he'd suggested she try freezing some meals and had even offered the spaghetti sauce recipe. He ran through that again. Tried to get it nice and conversational. I asked her if she needed any recipes, like I was thinking of the spaghetti one, because you can freeze that ahead, and maybe you and I (he'd point to Deena right then) could suggest a few things that would freeze well, because she was really struggling, he thought. Bringing Deena in like that would help, maybe, sort of make it public property. She wouldn't worry about it if he told her, he didn't think. And Christ, there wasn't anything wrong with helping somebody out, was there? He'd have to tell her soon, though, because she'd wonder why he waited, if he didn't.

Seven

SHE lay back in the tub, moderately comfortable at last. It had been no different this time. Paul had insisted it would be. "It hurt the first time," he had said, "but it won't anymore." She was sure she was bleeding. Flesh to flesh — how could there be such a sense of abrasion? And then the awful burning. Nerve centers gone crazy, pain in the groin, the legs, then even in the chest, too. Had the bathroom been further from the bedroom, she thought, she would have had to crawl the last few yards. She slid into the empty tub and gasped at the contact of the icy white porcelain on her skin. When she had caught her breath, she turned on the hot water, then watched it flow around and over her, climbing higher and higher till only her knees and breasts stuck up dry above it. The warmth had started her milk. She watched the thin white ribbons as they swirled gently along the surface of the water. She turned her knees to the side, slid them under, too.

And pain in the chest, what had caused that? Calm down, Paul had said. She was willing to admit it might be psychological — just the chest part, not the rest, but then there were interconnections, she was sure, ways in which parts of the body suddenly, strangely, linked up. And with sex, she knew, there was no logic or predictability. One more thing no one understood. Just as no one understood pregnancy. "We don't know what triggers labor." She placed her hand atop her abdomen. The water climbed to the top of her nipples, flowed over them, enclosed them. The hot water continued to pour onto, over her. It would be so nice, she thought, to stay in the tub till morning. To sleep there. But people died that way, she knew, just slipped under the surface of the water and drowned. She wondered why Marissa had objected so vigorously to her bath. Wasn't it like a return to the womb? She flattened her back against the bottom of the tub and watched her arms float to the surface of the water. Her fingers, like a collection of brittle sticks, seemed permanently extended, spread wide apart on the surface of the water. She must move carefully, she thought, to keep her arms from sinking to the bottom of the tub. Slowly, she edged herself forward, arms still afloat, lifted one hand, and turned off the hot water tap. Eddie, she thought, would have perspective — which Paul lacked — on this problem.

"Are you all right?" Paul asked as he poked his head in the bathroom door.

"Yes."

"You'll shrivel up to nothing," he said and laughed. A forced laugh, she thought. She had begun to wonder how she would get out of the tub. The bathroom was bound to be frigid compared to the water.

"Do you feel better?" he asked.

"Yes. But it still hurts."

"I'm sorry."

"It's not your fault," she said automatically.

"I guess it really is. I was the one who wanted to make love." She wondered if she would hear him if she slid all the way under water. She would need to come up for air sometimes.

"Do you think you should go to the doctor?" he asked.

"Why?"

"To see if there's anything wrong."

"I just had a baby," she said impatiently. She thought of papers tearing, of nails deliberately scraped across blackboards, and she shuddered.

"I know you had a baby recently. But from what he told you, from what it says in the books, we should be able to do it again by now. Maybe there's a complication." She slid down so the water lapped around her mouth. "If there's something wrong, we should know. It should be attended to. Sex or no sex." Her long hair fanned out around her head, floating along the water. "I mean, for your health. I care about your health. You should care about your health, don't you think?"

"Maybe I'm just tired," she said.

"Amy, this makes me very sad."

"I'm sorry," she said and turned her head from side to side, feeling the gentle pull the water had on her hair. "Maybe we'll never be able to do it again. What do you think about that?"

"It's not just our sex life, Amy. It's us."

"Paul, you should be on the soapies," she said, laughing. Her breath sent uneven ripples along the water's surface.

"Amy," he said. She watched his hand tightening its grip on the edge of the tub. "Amy." She didn't like his pajamas. White with little blue ovals like hundreds of tiny eyes. He never used to wear pajamas at all. "Would you," he whispered, "come out of there? Maybe we can talk in bed." She remembered a bath once, a long time ago, before they were married, no, not before they were married, but before Marissa was born, when they had taken a bath together. In a huge tub, with gold (they couldn't really have been gold, could they?) faucets. And it was their honeymoon, and Paul had lifted her out of the tub and carried her to the bed. Then he had covered her with two enormous amber-colored towels and rubbed her down.

She began to cry. Loud choking sobbing before she had even

realized it had begun at all. Paul pulled the plug, reached for her terry-cloth robe from the door, and flung it over his shoulder. He put his hands under her arms and began to pull her to standing. The purple velour flopped forward between their faces. He helped her from the tub, wrapped the robe round her and led her, still sobbing, to the bed. She turned her face into the pillow, and he attempted to pat her hair dry with a small towel.

"Amy," he said when she was finally quiet again, "I want you back." When she didn't answer, he added, "Do you remember how it used to be?" He stroked her head through the towel. "I'm not making it up, Amy. We had this baby because things were good between us. Because we thought it would add to our lives."

One thing she remembered: they had gone out for hot fudge sundaes two nights before Marissa was born. She turned over. "Things change," she said. "We're the grown-ups now." Each generation gets its turn, then steps down for the next. She thought she must have known that, even before it happened to her. What had been surprising was that it happened so suddenly. One minute she was Amy, the next minute a mother. At twenty it hadn't seemed that there were segments to life. There was just "being an adult." And it went on and on. When you got old, that was different. She could see that. You slowed down, you focused on grandchildren. That was different. But she had never thought that at twenty-six — twenty-six — a life could turn this suddenly. It was infantile, she knew, to try to turn the clock back. That's what her grandmother had always said, and she was right, there was no question about that. But she wished she had had an inkling back then of how it would be. She might have done things differently. But life had surprises. You had to roll with the punches, that was all. It was different for women because of that moment of birth. The pain ends, and there's a baby. The two phases so clearly delineated. Paul would accept things. He would come to see that a different life lay before them than the one they had envisioned. He would begin to understand about the animals, too. She had taken the collection of miniature Steiffs — the bear, donkey, rabbit, and kangaroo — tiny furry handfuls from the pages of A. A. Milne, and placed them on Marissa's windowsill. "I gave those to you," Paul had said. "We'll get other things for Marissa." But she had no use for them anymore. They were inappropriate in her life. Appropriate in Marissa's.

"Maybe you stay in too much," Paul said.

"Where can I go? I mean, with a baby?"

"Can't you visit someone?"

"Invite myself over somewhere?" Balancing a baby in her arms over the ice, with blankets, diapers, portable crib, and three changes of clothes for an hour-and-a-half visit. An unseen patch of ice, then, as she slips, falls, the baby slides from her arms and lands, smash, right where the car wheel paths have been shoveled out. Not in a snowbank. Right on the hard hard ground. Perhaps if she dressed her in Mrs. Martin's pink wool hat. Two hats, a blanket wrapped about her, but also round her head. "Avoid blows to the head at all cost." And how would she carry her? How would she keep the rotund bundle from rolling out of her arms? There would be nothing to grasp. Just roundness, roundness, roundness.

"You should get out yourself, then. Get someone to sit. Mrs. Martin, maybe. She's always begging to be able to stay with the baby. Come meet me for lunch, maybe."

"I can't."

"Why? What prevents you?"

"Lots of things. First, she's breast-fed. She won't take a bottle from you. I'm sure she won't take one from Mrs. Martin. So I'd worry about her the whole time, that she was screaming bloody murder. I'd rather stay here and know she's all right. And you can't really be serious about Mrs. Martin, can you? She shakes all over the place. I have to ask her to sit down before I'll hand her the baby. What'll I tell her, 'You just stay there now on the couch, I'll be back in three hours, but whatever you do, don't stand up?' And she's got great credentials, doesn't she, four dead babies."

"Amy, that's not her fault."

"How do you know? I won't leave the baby with her. I won't."

"Well invite someone here. Invite Ellen."

"I don't want Ellen. She's always asking me if I'm ecstatic because I have a baby."

"She just wants her own baby, you know that."

"And she wants me to promise her, swear it in blood, that when she finally does get a baby, life will be perfect. Well, it isn't, and maybe she ought to know that."

"So tell her."

"Nobody tells people things like that." She sat up in bed. "Not everybody has trouble. Maybe she won't. Maybe she wants a baby more than I did. Maybe her reasons are better for having one."

"Maybe you should talk to people who have children. See if they've had the same problems."

"I know what they say. They all say the same thing. This is the best time of your life. Wait till you have two. Don't rush things, all the same, everybody, everybody." She rubbed her hair vigorously with the towel.

"Don't we know anybody with babies the same age as Marissa?" She shrugged. "What about your roommate in the hospital?"

"I don't remember her name."

"Come on, Amy, you must."

"Paul, I didn't like her all that much. We were thrown together because we had both given birth. I didn't think I'd want to look her up afterwards."

"Sometimes you have to set aside certain issues. Maybe she didn't have the most compelling personality in the world, but she might give you some sense of her own position with an identical-aged baby. It's like a business arrangement. Not everyone I see at work is someone I would want to have as a friend, but I need to see each of them to solve certain problems."

"You don't have to ask them in for tea and have them spend the entire afternoon, though."

"No, but I do something equivalent, I suppose."

"I don't know her name."

"You can probably trace her through the hospital."

She tossed her towel toward the changing table, but it fell short, landing across a newly folded pile of diapers.

"Call the hospital," he reiterated. "What can you lose?"

"I didn't like her, Paul."

"She might help."

"She won't help, Paul." He lay back in bed, his hands clasped behind his head, his eyes closed. Amy turned off the light over the bed, then slid down under the covers.

"What do you think are good reasons for having a baby?" he asked.

"What do you mean?"

"You said you thought Ellen might have better reasons than you. That she might be better at it afterwards because of that."

"I don't know."

"No," he said. "I don't know either. What possible reasons could there be that aren't selfish? You want a baby for yourself, not for the baby's sake, right?" She said she supposed so. "There really are no good reasons, you know. It's irrational. At the risk of sounding a bit sappy, it's just part of the grand scheme."

"I thought we had reasons."

"We made up some reasons to justify our decision, that's all. But I don't think that makes us different from anyone else. I don't think there are any good, noble reasons to have a baby. For anyone. I think that's important to realize. It's not a good rallying point for guilt. I mean, whether we should have had a baby. We had one. It's done." She felt him turn toward her. "The corollary to that is that there are no bad reasons either, you know."

Would it be mean, she wondered, to ask Ellen what her reasons were?

"There are no good reasons," Paul said, "and no bad reasons."

Or, thought Amy, there simply are no good reasons. That was the fact, the rest was just Paul's rationalization for a deed already done. She might even warn Ellen. She might. But what if Ellen cried? What if she got defensive? What if she said Amy — well, she wouldn't say it, just imply it — was just a lousy mother? Christ, she wasn't going to say anything to Ellen. What a crappy idea.

Eight

ᏋDDIE visited every day for the next week. There was only one package, but still, he came every single weekday. Everything seemed to go well. Amy straightened the house in the morning while Marissa dozed, and then she made a list for the market. She ordered lunch and dinner ingredients, and the menus seemed suddenly to click together. There was an ease to it after the first few days. Paul was pleased. "Full-course meals," he commented. "Can't really complain, can I?" Everyone benefited.

Eddie brought little things some days from the bakery in Milton. A Napoleon one day, a huge chocolate brownie with a texture like rich fudge another day. She told him to stop after that because he came later when he detoured to Milton, but he still did it — a piece of marble cake with chunks of chocolate inside the next day, cupcakes with lemon filling after that — and, he arrived on time. "I do it first thing, now," he said. "It works in better. Also, it looks more like I'm stopping for breakfast that way. Nobody's going to question me for leaving the route that time of day."

On the day designated for the bath, she had prepared egg salad. Large-chunk egg, with freshly ground pepper and just a touch of curry. She ripped some lettuce from a newly delivered head and arranged a bed for the salad on each of two plates. Cherry tomatoes round the edge. She remembered to take off her fat sweater and tossed it across the bed.

When she served lunch, he asked her if she had place mats anywhere. Fumbling in the lower cabinets, she was able to hide her reddened face from his observation. Such ineptitude, she chastised herself as she reached under cookie sheets. No grace, no entertaining savoir faire. And after all that, plastic mats were all she could find. She wished she had a table cloth (had she ever had any round ones?), for the rectangles of plastic now seemed only awkward attempts at concealment of an ugly second hand table. Better yet, she wished she had a nicer table: a small antique, stripped oak piece. She wished Eddie had never seen that she had intended to feed him on the bare table. Or that, by extrapolation, she and Paul ate all their meals this way. The curry powder had seemed such a nice elegant touch, negated now by wood-grained formica.

"Much better," he said as he put their knives and forks on the shiny vinyl mats. He folded two paper napkins and set them under the forks. Embarrassment drained suddenly from her. She could feel it, like the sensation of a cold chill setting on, yet in reverse, rushing right out through the bottoms of her feet. Before, with their little teas, it hadn't been important that there be mats or napkins or any special routine or order. But today, when he was here without a package, it was. They were beginning something new together. Starting traditions, even. Was that sheer silliness, she wondered, calling place mats a tradition? Silly or not, it had sounded like a commitment. He would be back tomorrow, she knew.

"Are these new?" Paul would say to her that evening, his finger touching the primary-color abstractions on vinyl half hidden by his dinner plate. She would remind him they had bought them several years ago in Macy's, had used them only a few times and had forgotten them; found life less encumbered without them. "I like them," he would say. "It's nice to have some color in the room."

Eddie rocked the baby while Amy washed the dishes. "First thing about bathing," he said from his ice-cream parlor chair, "is to get everything you need before you start. Gather it together." She lifted the plastic tub from the top of the refrigerator and placed it on the counter next to the sink.

"Well, let's see," she said. "We need a washcloth, towel, soap, and shampoo. Anything else?"

"We'll skip shampoo today. We'll try that tomorrow." Tomorrow, she thought, and laughed aloud at her own accurate perceptions.

"Take a washcloth," he said, "and put it in the bottom, so she won't slide around." Amy went to fetch the items from the bathroom, and Eddie began to fill the tub. "You should fill the tub before you pick her up the first few times. I'm used to all this one-handed stuff," he said as he closed the tap. "You know how to test the water temperature, don't you?" He motioned for her to do so. She dropped some of the water on her wrist. "Maybe a little hot, just a little," she said.

He repeated the test himself. "Only the tiniest bit. In fact, it's really perfect, because by the time we undress her, it'll have cooled to exactly right." He carried Marissa to the changing table in the bedroom and began to undress her. "Marissa," he said softly to her, "you get to have your bath, you lucky creature. And splash and have a lovely time." He wrapped the naked baby in her bath towel and carried her to the tub. "You should get something to stick the pins in, Ame. Some kind of cushion thing. Then you know exactly where they are. They won't accidentally wind up stuck in the baby." Amy winced. "Towel over left shoulder," he said. "Then you know where that is, too." He looked directly at the baby as he said this, talking softly, as though he were telling it to her, not Amy. "Such a good baby," he said as he lowered her into the tub. He drizzled water from the washcloth onto the baby's belly, hands, and head. "I use very little soap," he continued in his croon to Marissa. Her hands danced slowly in front of her face, her mouth pursed up, and she stared intently at Eddie. "What does she need soap for?" he said, and gently caught one of her hands in his. "She's not ready for the sandbox yet, is she? Her little bottom needs soap, maybe, but really, at this age, the bath is for fun, isn't it, Missy? Just get you used to this part of life, that's all. Soon it's big-tub time, right, little doll?" And then he washed her head, rubbing it lightly, cupping her whole head with the washcloth, and then dripping the water again, up and down her belly. Her hands moved faster, making little splashes on their downswings. She seemed unaware they did so. He turned her gently over and washed her back and tiny buttocks. "The one trick for sure success," he said now, in a normal voice, "is to hold the corner of the towel under your chin." He demonstrated. "Then," he went on, "when you lift her out, you put her back up against the towel, and wrap one side, then the other round her, then pull the bottom of the towel up too. This part, the part under your chin," he said as he lowered the lime-green terry cocoon to his arms, "you use on her head. It forms a little hat." He lifted Marissa and kissed her forehead. "Such a good baby, not a sound," he praised her. Not a sound, Amy repeated to herself. Marissa seemed to have loved it. "Couple of weeks, she'll really be splashing in there. She'll drive you nuts with that. And as she — and you — get used to the bath, you can use more water. I used kind of a minimum today, just to get us going." Perhaps that's what had been wrong last time, Amy thought: too much water. Less was better.

Eddie rubbed Marissa's head gently. The baby's eyes closed, then opened, focusing firmly on Eddie's face. Amy touched the baby's cheek. How much more subdued than usual she seemed! "It's cold air, mostly, makes them miserable, so I always try to keep them covered as much as I can with the towel. Kind of change her under the towel. I sympathize, Missy," he said to the baby. "I feel exactly the same way when I get out of my shower. But when I win the lottery, my dear, I'm getting a heat lamp in the ceiling in the bathroom. And while I'm at it, I think I'll get a whirlpool with my winnings. Wouldn't that be something, my little baby," he crooned to Marissa, "whirlpool and heating lamp, and we'd never, never let my baby get cold, would we?" He handed her to Amy. "Tomorrow it'll be your turn."

"Thank you," she said.

"Now I'll run," he said, "and let you feed her." He stroked Marissa's head as Amy held her. "I'll see you tomorrow," he whispered (to the baby? to her? to both of them?). "Look how small that hand is," he said and kissed the baby hand that now, unconsciously and instinctively, twined itself round his finger. "Take care," he said. He was gone before she realized she might have protested his leaving.

"He'll be back," she said aloud when she had settled herself on the bed. She stroked Marissa's head as she nursed her. How the bath had softened that little bit of black hair! She rubbed her palm over and over across the top of the little head. She reached for one of the arms as they moved, just as they had in the bath, randomly before her face. The baby's hand opened as Amy touched it, then closed again round Amy's finger. Amy reached over to turn off the light, and the two of them settled deep into the pillows.

Nine

MARISSA'S arms shot out suddenly, almost convulsively, as Amy lowered her toward the plastic tub. She clutched Marissa to her chest, saving the little body from the touch of the water.

"What's wrong?" Eddie asked.

"What she did. That thing with her arms."

"Babies do that. That's just an old reflex left over from our monkey ancestry. They outgrow it. You'll miss it when it's gone."

"She didn't do it when you put her in the tub."

"She might have. It wouldn't have bothered me. I like that reflex. Makes them look so helpless and dependent. Try again," he said, pointing at the plastic tub.

"You do it, Eddie," she pleaded.

"The idea is for you to do it, Ame. I'm not here all the time. And I already know how to do it. You've got to stop letting her scare you. She's a baby, that's all. Try again."

The second time it was worse. The arms shot out in a larger circle, seemed to reach for something, anything, to save her, and Amy raised her up again. Marissa began to cry. "I think she's hungry," Amy said.

"I'm sure she's hungry, but we put her off yesterday, and she did fine. If you set up a new routine for her, she won't expect her milk till after the bath. Get her in the water this time. You only make her nervous with this up and down business."

Amy held Marissa out to Eddie. "You put her in," she said. "Then maybe I can do the rest." Eddie took a step back. "It'll be harder to transfer her in the tub than it will be for you to put her in initially. And she's getting cold, Ame." Amy closed her eyes and lowered the baby till she felt the water on both her arms. The baby continued to cry. "Did she do it that time, too?" Amy asked.

"Yes," Eddie told her, "but you're doing just fine now. Talk to her, so she'll stop crying."

But there was nothing to say. Each time Amy tried to open her mouth to say gentle little baby things, nothing came out. Eddie handed her the washcloth. She wet it in the warm bathwater then rubbed it gently over Marissa's belly. Still the baby cried.

"You're doing just fine," Eddie said softly from behind her, and she felt his hands lightly on her back. "Say, 'Pretty baby,' to her, Ame."

At first she couldn't get that to come out, either, but finally, on the third try, with Eddie rubbing her back, she said, "Pretty baby," very softly.

"Say it a couple of times," Eddie said.

"Pretty baby," she said, "pretty baby." The crying stopped for an instant, and the baby's eyes seemed to flash toward Amy. "Pretty baby," she said again, and she could feel that it almost sounded like Eddie's voice, kind of soothing, and the baby paused again. "You're a good girl," she said now, and Eddie's hands came to rest on Amy's shoulders. The baby stayed quiet while she rinsed her head and legs. When she turned her over in the water, the little cries began again, but stopped when Amy began to wrap her in the towel.

"I think that went very well," Eddie said. His hand encircled Amy's shoulder, as it had encircled Marissa's head the day before. Marissa's eyes looked up at the two of them. Amy stroked her head and watched her tiny little mouth, so soft and full. She leaned over and kissed the baby's mouth. Don't kiss the baby on the mouth, the doctor had told her that first day in the hospital. "The exchange of germs is phenomenal that way, and it's a bit odd, anyway, don't you think, parents and children kissing on the mouth?" She hadn't kissed her on the mouth till now. She kissed her again. "Pretty baby," she said and turned and smiled at Eddie.

"It went beautifully," he said.

"She cried," Amy said.

"Not the whole time. She may not cry at all next time, because you won't be so nervous. Anyway, babies should be allowed to cry. They can't talk. She just wanted to tell you she wasn't all that sure it was going to work out. But she feels better about it now, don't you, Missy?" He touched the baby's lips with his finger, and she smiled. "I'll clean up the bath stuff while you dress her," he said.

The phone rang while Amy was pinning the first side of the diaper. At the third ring, Eddie spoke from the kitchen. "I don't think I better answer it, Amy, do you?" She was startled.

"No, no, I'm coming." She carried Marissa, half dressed, with her. She looked toward Eddie as she reached for the phone. He turned away. It was Paul. At first she couldn't hear him, for Marissa began to cry, but Eddie took her from her arms and carried her into the living room, where he must have rocked her, because Amy heard no more crying.

"I've got you an appointment," Paul said.

"For what?"

"The gynecologist. He had a cancelation on Thursday."

"I don't want to go, Paul."

"I think we ought to check it out, honey."

"What will I do with the baby? How will I get there?" she asked, while she placed her fingers between the coils of the tele-phone wire. They alternated quite neatly, then, coil and knuckle, coil and knuckle.

"I'll take you. I'll hold Marissa in the waiting room."

"I don't want to go."

"Don't be infantile, Amy."

"He'll think I'm a hypochondriac."

"Either it hurts, or it doesn't, Amy. Does it hurt?"

"Yes," she growled, afraid Eddie might hear and comprehend all.

"It's for eleven o'clock Thursday. I just canceled a meeting and my luncheon date. That way, we can go out for lunch afterwards."

"With the baby?" she asked. "How?" Tears stung in her eyes. Eddie would not be able to come that day. "I'd better go, Paul, I'm standing here with Marissa only half dressed."

"Do you have a pencil?" he asked.

"Why?"

"I also called the hospital and got your roommate's name and phone number. You have a pencil?"

"Yes," she lied. She closed her eyes and ran her fingers along the coiled wire, stretching it out and releasing it while he gave her the information.

"Give her a call, OK?"

"When I get a chance," she said.

"I'll see you later," he said and hung up.

Eddie stood at the door to the kitchen now. He had pulled his shirt from his pants and wrapped Marissa in its long front ends. "You didn't have to stay out there," she said.

He shrugged. "I didn't mind," he said. She held her hands out for Marissa.

"I won't be here Thursday," she said. "Paul has something he thinks I should do."

He unwrapped the baby and handed her to Amy. "He's your husband, darlin'," he said and touched her face lightly with both his hands. Like this, face to face, she could see directly into his eyes. The baby whimpered, and one infant hand attached itself to the fabric of Amy's shirt. Another random gesture.

"She's getting cold, Amy," he said and moved closer, sheltering the infant with his presence.

"I'll dress her. It's the doctor," she said. "He wants me to see the doctor again." Eddie stood in the doorway of the bedroom while Amy dressed Marissa. "We've . . . I . . ." Eddie was right about the pins. They were dangerous lying about this way. And she was so damnably disorganized. Things were scattered about here and there. Like now, where were the clean undershirts? Anyway, how absurd, long-sleeved undershirts. Her sister had written to say the long-sleeved undershirts Amy wanted for the layette were unavailable in Maryland. "Do you really mean long-sleeved," she had written, "or just sleeves, as opposed to sleeveless?" She pulled the tiny shirt closed across Marissa's body. So, Joe, she would have liked to have said, did you and your wife have sexual problems after your kids were born? "Eddie," she said, "Does it really get easier, or do you say that to me so I won't commit suicide in despair?"

He came and stood next to the changing table. "It gets easier, Ame. My wife and I were very young when our first was born. We hadn't been married very long. Nobody tells you how hard it is. But it is." He watched while she slipped Marissa's foot into a stretch suit. "She told me a long time later that she thought the marriage was over then. That she'd never be my girl again. We were really young, Ame. I thought the same thing. I felt cheated."

"Paul and I, we aren't . . ." she began, and felt the intended word, *lovers,* catch momentarily on her tongue then scatter, like a child's beads dropped on a kitchen floor. She had not wanted him to know. Perhaps the noise of the bouncing word-beads would distract him. And you and I, she thought, while the multicolored beads popped and crashed into cabinets and linoleum, and you and I? Could we, would we? She closed her eyes and envisioned their hands entwined, endlessly curving and enclosing one another. A weakness in the thighs, a slight shaky feeling in the lower legs, and she sat on the bed, Marissa in her arms. Between us: Marissa. The beads had almost stopped, a few odd ones rolling still into distant corners and crevices of the room, and she noticed he had retucked his shirt. She shouldn't have told him. Shouldn't have even hinted at such failings.

"We'll skip Thursday, then," he said, and her fingers, seeing his fingers empty, closed more tightly around the baby. "It's difficult to have a baby," he said at the door. His hand stroked her arm. "It seems so difficult now, but it clears up, believe me. You'll have your life again," he said. She buried her head against Marissa and let her tears soak into the terry stretch suit. "I promise," he said, and his hand tightened on her arm. She reached an arm round him, leaned her head on his chest. "I promise," he said and stroked her hair. "I promise."

Futures, somedays, and promises, she thought later, as she nursed Marissa. She leaned her head back and laughed quietly, the memory of the firmness of his back still under her hand. Amy moved Marissa to the other breast. The baby mouth closed round the nipple and began its fierce little pulling. She felt its tug all the way to her womb. Will we be lovers, she wondered, Joe and I?

On some nights, Amy felt there was a ferocity to Paul's sleep. He battled with the blankets, clutching them round himself. It would be a brief struggle, for after only moments he would be soundly asleep. Those nights he never said good-night. The lights would still be on, and Amy would be just settling into bed, perhaps not even in bed yet, and his rhythmic snoring would have begun. The first few times it had happened — the first year they were married

— she had cried. His violent somnolence left no place for her as a sleeping or sexual partner. Didn't he love her anymore? she would demand the next morning. He thought it funny that she could get so upset about it, for he had absolutely no memory of his thrashing or teeth grinding. He could recall no dreams for her, although he admitted once that his jaw was inexplicably sore. She slept little those nights; the darkness seemed too powerful, too great a force to leave unwatched. There would be a certain amount of discomfort, for she would rigorously adhere to her side of the bed, unwilling to touch Paul in any way. The fierceness, the thrashing, were characteristics so rarely seen, she was never fully able to identify them with Paul. There was a stranger in the bed those nights.

The night before the doctor's appointment, he did it again. She decided to keep the light on. At least for a time. Once she had seen he was irrevocably asleep, she took the notebook and pen from the desk and brought them into the bed with her. "Today," she wrote, "I shampooed her. She cried very little. I like to feed her right after the bath because she's softer, more relaxed. It may just be that she's tired out. She would not write that Eddie had stayed while the baby nursed. She had begun to feed Marissa before Eddie finished putting the bath things away. He had come into the living room, and, instead of passing through and out the door, he had sat down on the couch. His previous embarrassed protestations lingered like unattended cobwebs which he seemed to monitor earnestly by gazing from one upper corner of the room to the next. He hadn't been able to look at her, at the baby, at the nursing, but that would come. The baby had been drowsy when she finished feeding and he had reached out for her, then held her till she was fully asleep. At the door he had kissed Amy on the cheek and said only, "See you Friday." She put her own hand now on her cheek and slid her fingers slowly across her face, across her own lips. "Tomorrow," she wrote in the notebook. But tomorrow, she thought, I go to the doctor. Then there was nothing else to write. She would turn the light out after all. She propped her pillow behind her, in order to sit up slightly. She would keep her eyes open as long as possible. In the dark a phrase came to her: I'm starting to like her. But she would not write that; would not commit to paper implications of lack of previous affection. "Her hair smells lovely and feels so soft," she whispered. She turned on the light. On the same page, the one about the shampoo, she wrote about her infant's hair.

The inscription under Eddie's high school yearbook picture was, "A friend to all, but a sweetheart to one." His picture was on the page next to Deena's, and she had sketched a chain of flowers to link their portraits. There were wreaths of flowers round them both. What he had liked about it was that you could tell each flower variety. That's the kind of artist she was. You could say, there's a daisy, there's a marigold, there's a rose. And she hadn't even used any color. Under her picture it said "Pretty as a rose, but already picked." Deena's mother had been annoyed about that one. She said it sounded tacky and couldn't understand how Deena had allowed it. Deena explained that a committee had chosen the sayings, and she hadn't had anything to do with it, and besides, it just meant she was spoken for, that's all.

"*Spoken for* is fine," Mrs. Svenden said, "it's *picked* I don't like. Makes me think of fruit, picked over, lying in the market."

"It means selected, Mrs. Svenden," Eddie had finally interjected. "Not left over." He remembered how he had felt like putting his arm round Deena then but hadn't. Mrs. Svenden wouldn't have liked it.

Then that same night his father had handed him his graduation present. It was a check with the words "For college tuition" written right on the front. "I'm going to get a job," he told his father, but his father had said, "You're just fixing to get married, and you're too young. Much too young."

"It's not because of marrying her that I want a job, but because I want to work, not go to school, that's all."

"Eddie," his mother had whispered to him later in the kitchen, "he meant it as a gift, not a punishment." He still held the check, although he'd run it through his hands a lot while they had argued and had even crumbled it at one point and made a fist with the check sticking up out of it, but now he took it and smoothed it out against the edge of the table, then turned it around and smoothed it on the other side so it didn't curl but lay flat. He took out his wallet and put the check inside. Then he went into the living room, where his father sat, and thanked him.

It was one year out of his life, he figured. His father hadn't said anything about four years. One year. And he'd work while he was in school. He'd put away all the money, and they'd get married just as soon, anyway.

His father crowed with pleasure over his first-semester transcript and handed him ten dollars. "Take your little girl friend out for a pizza," he said. In February he took the civil service exam. In June he went to visit Mr. Svenden to ask if he could marry Deena. By then a place had opened at the post office. "And college?" Mr. Svenden asked, as his own father would, later that same evening.

"This is what I want to do," he said. "Be a mailman. College won't help me do that."

"One winter," Mr. Svenden said, "and you'll be wishing for the nice warm classroom again."

Eddie had smiled but had said no more.

"If your mind's made up then," Mr. Svenden had said, "I won't say no to you. I know you'll take care of her."

When they were married, Eddie asked Deena to give up her job at the florist shop. He had no objections to her working, that wasn't it, but he wanted her to be there when he came home. So he'd "feel married," he told her. There was plenty for her to do in the house, she said. She wanted to make curtains and practice baking, and she didn't mind at all, not if he didn't think they needed the money. He said, no, they could manage without — it was more important for her to be there. He liked making love in the late afternoon, and his job brought him home earlier than lots of other jobs might have. Deena always had flowers on the table at dinner. Nice arrangements that she got at special prices because of the friends she had at the flower shop.

One afternoon she told him, "I want everyone to know we sleep together."

"Don't you think they already do? Isn't that what you're supposed to do when you're married?"

"I don't think all married people do, though," she said. "They try it, maybe, and they don't like it or something, and they stop doing it."

He told her she was crazy. And then the next afternoon while they were making love her mother called to invite them for dinner, because she'd made double pot roast, and he'd whispered to her, while she was still on the phone, come on now, tell her, if you want her to know so badly, tell her, and Deena had gotten off, and she'd been furious and hit him with the pillow, and then she'd said, I meant, I want to have a baby, I want to walk around big and fat and pregnant, so everybody knows you and I sleep together. Like a big sign round my neck, saying Eddie loves Deena. A little love token. And they'd made love again, only this time they didn't use anything. And they didn't use anything after that, and she had her positive pregnancy test on her twentieth birthday.

He used to say to her, then, after Elizabeth was born, "Sweetheart to two," and one time he said it and she cried and asked him, do you love her more than me? And he'd said, no, but later he'd thought, maybe I do, but only in a funny little way, because Deena's still my wife and Elizabeth is my baby, but he had wondered, because it was such an intense feeling he had for that baby. But it was different, he decided. He didn't think it was right to even think of them together like that anymore, so he didn't say that bit about two sweethearts, but then as they had more and more girls, Deena took it up, saying "sweetheart to four," and then five, and so on. She found it amusing once she was older. Once she saw, he guessed, babies were babies, and wives were wives.

Ten

$\mathscr{P}$AUL sat on a white wicker chair. Amy sat across the waiting room from him on a contemporary interpretation of a Windsor. Both chairs were softened by cushions in bright print fabrics. Even so, not very comfortable in pregnancy. A woman seated next to Amy had her legs spread wide round the front of another Windsor chair, allowing room for the massive full-term weight she carried. Amy had sat in that same chair two months earlier, the afternoon before Marissa was born. She had squirmed and shifted, she remembered, actually fighting back tears of discomfort by the time the nurse brought her to the examining room. "All I want to do is lie down," she had said to her as they walked down the corridor to an examining room. The nurse had been apologetic about the crowds in the office. One of the doctors had been called to an emergency, she said. Women "near the end," she laughed, were very, very touchy. But she didn't mind — that just made the job interesting, she said. So many, many phases to each pregnancy! Besides, she added, it was a good sign. It meant Amy would be "going" soon.

Amy's hand drifted across her abdomen, as it had so often before in this waiting room. She was the only woman in the room now without a belly. The full-term woman flung her magazine down with a loud sigh. An abortive call for help. The receptionist would never hear it behind her glass partition. And she had begun to shift about, seeking, Amy knew, the unattainable position where the baby's weight would not press on nerve or bladder. Paul riffled through the pile of *American Baby* and *Good Housekeeping* and settled into a copy of *Twin Cities*. Marissa slept on Amy's lap. The only woman in the room with a baby. The prize they all awaited.

Paul had been right. They had decided to have a baby for fun. Well, there really was nothing wrong with it as a concept, was there? Shouldn't making babies be a pleasure? And it had been, letting that sperm, after all the years, go free; swimming toward its natural destination. And waiting, waiting for weeks to see if their efforts had been fruitful. And when they weren't, the disappointment was so real that they had wept together. They wept for a lost, never-conceived child. They bemoaned the lost time, the years of their youth wasted on joyous lovemaking, rather than reasoned conception. But each month, they were sparked anew by the prospect of getting the gametes connected. They read pregnancy books together in bed, then followed, sometimes in earnest, sometimes in laughter, the exhortations for him on top, her on top, deep penetration, shallow penetration, abstention from coffee, indulgence in two ounces of wine before retiring. One might increase the chances of conception, they read, by abstention for a number of days before ovulation. This advice they ignored, opting instead for what Paul termed "maximum saturation." Eventually, it worked. The gametes connected, the explosion occurred.

"I'm not ready," she had said to the doctor the last afternoon of her pregnancy.

"Ten lunar months hasn't been long enough for you?" he had asked as he stripped the filmy white glove from his right hand. "I think you'll go on your own in the next day or two, but if not, I'll want to see you Friday. We'll consider inducing then, because you've gone considerably beyond your date." He lifted papers in the manila folder and let them flutter over his fingertips. "That baby's ready." He closed the folder. "Go home and pack," he said as he went out the door.

She had cried all the way home. It was supposed to culminate this way, with a baby, wasn't it? The secret seed was about to turn willful, to begin on its own. And between here and there, she found herself moaning aloud in the car, were stirrups, scissors, scalpels, blood, and polished (to blinding) delivery room tile. Knock, knock, the baby would say, and whether she wanted it or not, a rush of hormones would trigger the swing of otherwise rigid, bony structures. Breathe, someone would chant. Bear down, another would command, and it would be done.

"Gravity," the childbirth instructor had intoned, "was the mid-wife of the primitive woman. Squatting over a little nest of straw, the pull of the earth would ease the baby from the womb." Breathe rhythmically, now, and all pain will dissolve. A peak moment, the all-time natural high. "We could have another one right away, if you like," Paul had said. "Get it all over with all at once, you know."

"Time for delivery," the doctor had finally announced. Amy had grabbed for his hand on one side, for Paul's on the other. "Don't make me go," she had begged, breaking the fragile rhythm of her breathing. But the bed continued to roll, out the door, down the hall, her hands still grabbing the hands of the two who walked beside her.

"They're usually relieved," the doctor explained to Paul over the bed. "It means it's almost over." The doctor had leaned down toward Amy. "It's almost over," he said. "You'll have your baby in just a few minutes." Then she had begun crying in earnest. The nurse, the one who had been so nice, had tried to get her breathing

going again. Amy would not cooperate. The pain was no worse
without the breathing. It was unbearable either way.

And she didn't want to watch in the mirror. She wouldn't watch
herself splitting open. "It's a lovely little girl," the doctor said,
but a twisted blue cord blocked her view as they held the creature
up. "What's her name?" the doctor asked. Amy couldn't remember what they had decided. "Marissa," Paul said.

"Beautiful name," the doctor said. The nurses agreed. Amy
wasn't sure. Perhaps a new name, one they just started to think
about, would be better. The ones from pregnancy didn't seem right
now. That white, white baby didn't seem a Marissa. And she was
smaller than Amy had imagined. Her limbs were thin and elon-
gated. A new name, she thought, would be far better.

They hadn't wanted her to hold the baby while she was being
stitched up. Just as well. Paul held her. The inside of Amy's mouth
was so dry, her tongue could no longer recognize its texture as
familiar. Fascinated now, she watched in the mirror, where she had
not been able to before, while the doctor stitched. Putting the
pieces back together, she thought, making me new. The nurse
brought her ice water.

"When does it hurt?" the doctor asked.

"During intercourse," she said. She'd told him that already in
his outer office. Lying here, with her legs in those stirrups, with
that nurse smiling from ear to ear at her, she thought the least he
could do was remember what she had told him five minutes before.
If she didn't have to talk, it didn't seem quite so degrading to be
in that position.

"At entry?" he asked.

"Yes. But not just then." She'd need to clarify, of course. Having come this far, she might as well get an accurate diagnosis.
"The whole time. Then afterwards, too. An abraded feeling, kind
of."

Again he stripped the white glove from his hand. "Everything's healing well. There isn't any kind of damage. I suspect what you have is just some excessive dryness in there." She remembered the foreign feel of her mouth after childbirth. "It sometimes happens with nursing mothers. It's related to a condition known as senile vaginitis. I can give you an estrogen suppository that will improve the condition. But sometimes it's absorbed."

"What does that mean?" she asked.

The nurse whispered, "You can take your feet out now, Mrs. Gold," and she disappeared out the door. The doctor offered her his hand, she reached for it, and he drew her up to sitting.

"There are sometimes traces in the breast milk."

"Is it bad for the baby?"

"Probably not in the dose she would get. The other treatment is to curtail the breast-feeding. That will clear it up. It's a situation which calls for priority setting. Some women decide to continue nursing, but for a limited time, through three months, say, and simply abstain from intercourse if it's uncomfortable during that time. When the husband and wife are both committed to the nursing, they find that an appropriate solution. You have to work it out together. But you're looking fine," he said after a pause. "Just fine. I'll get you a prescription."

"Thank you," she said automatically.

At the pharmacy, they argued about the ice-cream festival.

"It's too cold for the baby, standing around like that," Amy said.

"She's always inside," he said. "You've got to give her a chance to adjust to the climate. I see babies out all the time, looking red-cheeked and happy. A guy in my office says he buys down snowsuits for his kids."

"Marissa doesn't have a down snowsuit."

"Amy, you're in too much with her. The way to build up her resistance — and yours — is to start getting out. The ice-cream festival's a tradition in St. Paul. You can't keep fighting these things if you're going to live here. You've got to start becoming part of the culture, winter and all."

"I don't consider a bunch of lunatics eating ice-cream cones outdoors in ten-below weather to be culture. It's just silly and exhibitionistic."

"People need to do it. To flaunt the cold, to show themselves and everyone else that they won't let the elements get them down."

"You know, Paul, people don't have to do this in other parts of the country. They don't have to prove they can eat ice cream, or breathe, or whatever, in subzero weather. Because there isn't any subzero weather. They just live their lives in relative comfort."

"Didn't we used to have fun skiing? I always thought you enjoyed it."

"On vacations, Paul, on weekends in Vermont. It contrasted with our lives, and besides, that was before she was born."

"I manage to walk to work every day. I don't use the tunnels."

"I understand they give honorary degrees sometimes to non-natives who show exceptional imperviousness to the weather. I'm sure you must be a candidate." She shifted Marissa from one arm to the other.

"I know it's cold. I simply don't know of any other way to deal with it. I work here. We live here. How else can we behave and stay sane through these cold months?"

"It's just that she's young, Paul. Maybe next year. What will it really prove to take her out in below-zero weather?"

"What about you?" he asked.

"I'll survive," she said. "You can't cross-country ski with a baby, Paul."

She considered: if she were to stretch out both her hands to the side, in the middle of the aisle, and if she picked up precisely the right speed, could she get the contents of the shelves from both sides to fly in front of her arms? And could she, running and engaged that way on both sides, muster enough accelerative force to get the multitudinous boxes and bottles to arc upward at the end of the shelves rather than simply plop off the end? The upward arc was important. Paul would stop talking about snowsuits. She would need both hands free, but she felt herself suddenly balking at handing Marissa over to Paul. She didn't want to hand Marissa to Paul in order to do it. She didn't ever want to hand Marissa to Paul anymore. He never seemed to take it seriously when she told him to make sure he supported the baby's head. She tapped her finger along the tops of deodorants, dandruff shampoos, toothpaste, razor blades, and dental floss. At the foot powder, she paused and said aloud, but very softly, "Joe, it isn't my fault, is it?"

"What?" Paul asked, turning back toward her.

"Nothing," she said. Nothing, nothing, nothing. Her hand moved through the stationery goods now and lighted on an extra-fine-point fountain pen. It might be even better than the one she had at home. "I need a pen," she said, laying it carefully on his already open checkbook. She walked to the front of the store and waited with Marissa till his transaction was complete.

When he started the car, he tried once more. "What do you think? You think you want to go to the festival or not?"

Why was she unable to make herself understood? Hadn't she told him somewhere in that conversation that she wouldn't go?

"Would you want to go?" he tried again.

"She'll need to eat soon," Amy said in what she knew was her final attempt at indirect persuasion.

"We won't stay long. Then we can go back to the house for lunch."

Everything has changed. Life is different now, she thought. Life is different. When she got home later, she would write that phrase in her notebook. She remembered the reflective lamp in the delivery room. The student nurse had adjusted it badly, and it had shone directly into her eyes. It had been impossible to resist by that time. The immobile joints had swung open all of their own accord. Thy will be done. And my own will, she thought, ground finer than dust, was dispersed into the air of the delivery room, then quickly inhaled in that one frantic newborn cry. The one that made everyone laugh and smile. No longer Amy's will. Now Marissa's. And then they handed it back to her, wrapped in a pink receiving blanket. New generation. New person. Begin again. She drew the pen from the paper bag that lay on the front seat, removed the cap, and stroked the fine sharp point. Life is different. If he didn't know it, at least she did.

She nursed Marissa at the kitchen table while Paul ate his sandwich. She would skip the bath today. It wasn't as though Marissa played in the sandbox or anything. One missed day wasn't a tragedy in filth. "I thought I might call Ellen this afternoon and see if she'll drop by," she said to him. He smiled at her in silence. She heard a heavy truck rumble by the front of the house. What if Eddie had a package today? Would he bring it anyway? Touch his hand to his cap, smile at Paul over her shoulder, and back out the door? What if Paul wanted to answer the door? Would it make Eddie defensive? Angry? She wondered if Eddie ever got angry.

"Why don't you call her now?" Paul asked.

"It can wait, Paul. I'll do it after you go back to work. Marissa needs the other breast, anyway."

"I'll hold her, you can call."

"No," she said menacingly.

"I was trying to be helpful, Amy." She cupped her hand round the baby's head. She bent her own head and kissed Marissa's lips.

He stood and began clearing the table. Dishes scraping on a porcelain sink made her flesh creep. "See you at dinner," he said, and headed toward the front of the house.

"You were the one who called her lightweight," she said through the door, after he had gone. "And flyaway, too, that was your term, not mine," she said on her way back to the kitchen.

Ellen was a little puff of dandelion gone to seed, just waiting to be blown sky-wide with the first passing child's breath. Poor Ellen, she thought, remembering her panic the summer day Amy had arrived for lunch to be greeted by the bitter smell of burned food. There was Ellen running (fluttering? Amy considered) round and round the kitchen, poking at her casserole and paging rapidly through her cookbook. Then she'd turned round — firm suddenly — and said, "I'll take you out to lunch."

"You don't have to," Amy had said. "We can just relax and have a can of tuna fish with a little lemon juice on it. I don't need anything fancy. Some toast with it, maybe, that's all." Ellen stood at the sink, scraping blackened layers off what she had described on the telephone that morning as "fettuccine done a new way," and Amy said, "Or we could eat that, I'm sure it's all right inside, don't you think?" But Ellen had turned the casserole upside down over the sink, letting the whole mass plop indelicately against the porcelain. "I'd rather you'd just let me take you out," Ellen said as she ran the water over and through the maze of noodles below. "I can't sit here smelling this anymore."

"All right," Amy said. "We can go out."

"And I pay," said Ellen.

"And you pay," Amy said, adding under her breath, "whatever you want, and whatever you need."

"She sounds nutty," Paul had said when she told him about the afternoon. "It makes me jumpy to be with her. Can't we avoid them?"

"Poor Ellen," Amy had said, and Paul had groaned, recalling their visit to the Chamberses' when Ellen had done nothing but apologize for her messy house. Amy and Paul had thought it looked immaculate — and had told her so, repeatedly. "And remember their tour?" he asked. Introduction to Discount Living in the Midwest, he called it.

"It's because she can't get pregnant," Amy had said.

"Whatever it is, it's gotten out of hand," Paul said.

Now he was the one pushing for her to get the friendship going again. They had nothing in common. Nothing to share. Amy had known that from their first afternoon together.

We'd be quite a team, Ellen and I, she thought. Two great nitwits. She couldn't bear the thought of sitting across the table from her now, listening to her discourse on her favorite topics of bargains and ovulation. She doesn't need conversation, anyway, Amy thought. She needs hand holding and head patting. Amy wasn't in the mood for that. "I wish I could be like you," Ellen had said. "You're so together, so calm."

Amy flung the last lunch plate into the sink and saw it crash against two beverage glasses, shattering them both. She began to count the tiny slivers that sparkled up at her, reached thirty-seven, and saw there were too many pieces to ever get an accurate reckoning. She lowered herself slowly to the floor, and sitting, back against the cabinet, she told herself, maybe I'll just write her a letter.

She remembered rain. What was so nice about rain was that you could hear it. You didn't always have to look out the window to find out if there was rain the way you did with snow. You could hear it on the roof, even though you were on the first floor. You could hear it on the overhang over the back steps and on the peak over the front steps. And you could hear it splashing on itself out in the puddles in the street.

"Didn't snow at all this week, did it?" Paul said as he walked in the house that evening. "Now do you think that's a good sign or a bad sign?"

"What do you mean?"

"Did it not snow because it was simply too cold for snow, or because we're headed into spring?"

"It's too cold for snow."

"The days are getting longer."

When there was a very heavy rain, she remembered, and it let up — not necessarily even completely stopped — the birds would begin to sing and chatter to one another from the trees. And when the rain did stop, they swooped down from the trees, back and forth between them (celebrating the end of the wet? drying their wings?) and then they regathered on the lawns, pecking about for worms brought to the surface for their pleasure by the storm. Then you smelled the grass and the seeds.

"Have you noticed," said Paul as he hung his jacket in the closet, "that it's staying light later?"

Amy glanced toward the window. There was a small area not covered with ice, off to the right upper corner of each window, but it was no larger or smaller than yesterday. Or than last week. "Not warmer," she said.

"No, but once the days start getting longer, the earth starts heating up more, retaining more heat. It's a good feeling. Encouraging." She walked to the window, peered through the peek hole. "There was light in the sky when I left work today. Not a lot, but some. I'm not leaving work in the dark anymore," he said as he settled into the corduroy chair.

"How much snow is there?" she asked, still at the window. "More than four feet, isn't there?"

"I guess. Last year there were fifty-seven inches."

They were always warning you on the news to clear it from flat roofs and from against windows. "It'll be May before it's gone," she said. "Could it last till June, do you think?"

"The sun gets pretty strong by April, I think. The snow should be gone by May first."

"Even here?" she asked. "Even here the sun is strong?"

"Eventually. Like I said, the earth gets warmer as the days get longer. Don't you remember last summer?" She remembered Mrs. Martin, with her shades pulled down, with the smell of heated Victorian carpet, the smell of dry dust rising as she walked across it, greeting her. It was happening to her in her own apartment now. Closed windows, overheated rooms. It was difficult to breathe such dry air all the time. When would they open the windows again? There was always a smell now, yet she could not track it down. Baby smells? Garbage smells? Paul didn't smell it. Her mucous membranes, baked hard and claylike, must have their own smell now. It was with her all the time.

"What's for dinner?"

But she had forgotten this time. What with writing the letter to Ellen, which, in the end, she had only ripped up, anyway, because she had kept writing phrases like "I hate to say this" and "I'm sorry to say," with no content in between. Ellen wouldn't want to read it, nobody would want to read it. Amy didn't even want to reread it. And then she'd had to nurse Marissa again. "I've been thinking of egg rolls all day," she said.

"That's not a bad idea," he said. "We haven't had a takeout treat in a while. And it's good timing because it's not snowing. What are you supposed to do with that medication?" he added without pause. "Did you start using it already?"

She had forgotten about that, too. "No," she said. "He didn't really explain. I'll have to try to decipher the instructions."

"I'll take a look at it," he said. "Where is it?"

She couldn't remember putting it down anywhere. "I might have left it in the car," she said.

"Amy . . ."

"I did have the baby, you know. Why didn't you think to carry it in?"

"OK," he said. "I forgot, too. I'll get it when I go to get the food."

"Thank you," she said. She wondered if it would have a little label on it warning against freezing, the way some prescriptions did. If so, it would be unusable now, left as it had been in the car for so many hours. She watched the lights of the car as Paul backed it down the drive. They caught in the web of ice in the kitchen window. The ice seemed to glow for a few moments even after she knew the car was further down the drive.

Eleven

*T*HE medication hadn't really helped. Paul thought maybe as they contined to make love it might begin to take effect, but she had cried, and he had withdrawn, rolled over and gone to sleep. It was true that the pain hadn't been quite as severe as the other times, but then they hadn't done it for as long this time. And maybe the medication did improve it, but just not enough to make it comfortable. And pleasurable? That was a joke. What was the use? she thought, when the warnings in the pharmaceutical literature indicated that Marissa would now probably have cancer of the uterus at fourteen because Amy had used the product. Priorities. Paul thought she should use more of it. Or stop nursing. Those were his priorities. She took her new pen and underlined the word *senile* every time it occurred in the literature that had come with the suppositories. Over and over. Senile membranes. I never had the luxury of growing old, she thought. I just am old. And how did Paul know, or how even did the doctor know, that she would be restored if she were to stop nursing? Some changes were irreversible. What guarantees did she have that this wasn't one of them? If she stopped nursing and sex was still impossible, there would be no way to resume the nursing. No one would have gained anything. And why hadn't she ever heard about this "condition" before? The doctor had acted as if it were common. He hadn't mentioned it or warned her about it before pregnancy, before childbirth. No one ever mentions the bad things. Never, never, never. No women mentioned it. Perhaps she was the first case. The doctor's calm, matter-of-fact presentation might have been complete sham. "It's nothing to worry about," they liked to say. They were always trying to prevent hysteria in their offices.

Marissa had wakened at four-thirty, rather than six, this morning. Amy had fed her and put her back down. Surprisingly, she had gone back to sleep, but now at five-fifteen, Amy didn't want to sleep anymore. She crawled back into bed. Paul slept soundly. Almost seven hours till Eddie comes, she thought. If Marissa hadn't wakened her as early as she had, she wouldn't now have so many waking hours to get through. But she had plans, at least. She was going to serve deli-style sandwiches for lunch and cut up cold vegetables to go with them. She'd order it all from the market, first thing. And a spicy sauce to dip the vegetables in. A fruit salad for dessert. Wouldn't jazz flute be nice, too, she thought. She hadn't played any records lately.

He was prompt. At twelve, when he arrived, Marissa was asleep and they sat right down to their lunch. He said she shouldn't have made so much work for herself, but that it really did look beautiful. He sat in a chair and watched while she bathed Marissa. She told him how she used to play the flute when he said he liked the record she had on. "I'll miss you till Monday," she said to him when he was leaving. He kissed her hand. Monday, she thought, as he walked out the door, she would make hamburger au poivre.

On Monday he brought her a dark chocolate candy bar. They broke off pieces and shared it while she fed Marissa. He said he thought she ought to set up the playpen. "It'll give you more freedom," he said. "She'll be able to look at all the toys hanging on the sides, and that'll keep her amused. Maybe only a few minutes at first, but it'll get longer after a while. Gets her used to it, too. For when she's older and you need to keep her safe and out of trouble sometimes." The next day he helped her set it up. They hung a ring of colored keys, a Raggedy Ann, and a dog-shaped music box from the mesh of the sides, and then suspended a crib gym set over the center. When they put Marissa down on the floor of the playpen, she lay quietly, staring and moving her head slowly from side to side. After a while her arms began to circle about slowly, then more and more rapidly. She hit herself occasionally in the face. She would slow down, lie quietly again for a while, and then the arms, and even the legs, would begin flying about. They watched her, laughed at her, and ate their lunch together. After twenty minutes, Marissa was so exhausted, she disintegrated into frantic tears. Amy carried her to her crib, and she fell asleep immediately.

Three days later Eddie pointed out that the motions seemed less random. Amy saw what he meant. She seemed to reach upward now, always missing the gym set, of course, but the rotary motions seemed less dominant. A few days after that they both gasped simultaneously when she reached for and touched the gym set. And again she reached for it, sending the red bead dangling wildly. Eddie held his open hand out toward Amy's, and they clasped tightly. Three more times Marissa made the red bead swing, and then the rotary motions returned. "Such miracles," Eddie said, shaking his head. He kissed the side of her hand before he let it go.

She tried the medication once more then threw it out. Paul suggested she visit her sister. She refused. She couldn't. She would miss Eddie.

"There's a baby," Eddie said to her one day the following week, "over on Ralston Street. Teeny little thing. Born a month early. Mother's very young. Maybe twenty, I'd say."

"Joe," she murmured, and she could see the teapot sway in her hands.

"A little boy," he said. He held Marissa on his lap while he spoke. "What'd Marissa weigh when she was born?"

"Seven pounds even," she said.

"This one was just barely five. Can you imagine how small that is?"

"No," she said and turned her face away.

"Sometimes they can't even get clothes to fit such little ones. They just seem to drown in all the extra folds of the fabric. Supposed to go above freezing tomorrow," he said after a pause.

"Joe," she said aloud.

"You're funny," he said and touched her hand lightly.

That evening her sister Julia called. "Are you very cold out there?" she asked. Through the phone wires, Amy heard the wavering, gravelly quality that was so much like her mother's voice. "All the winter things are on sale here," Julia continued. "The spring things are in. Do you need anything?" It is Julia, she reminded herself. I have no mother. "I saw some nice flannel pajamas today."

"Yes," Amy said.

"It's still cold, then?" in Mama's voice again. Do you know, Julia, that you have Mama's voice?

"Horrible," Amy said, and the word hung, an unfinished, undirected phrase addressed to no one. The nomenclature *mommy, mama, mother* rushed by quickly and her tongue longed to stab out to retrieve one of the words just as the frog, in one sudden, almost invisible motion, will ensnare an insect. The flyby of words was over before she could react. *Julia* drifted by more slowly now, and she reached, ready to bite at it, capture it, but her mouth could only move soundlessly, teeth edging round the word, and she heard the solemn, lonely *horrible* echoing directionlessly.

"Horrible," she said again, forcing her voice to make it sound a phrase, a sentence, a communication or completed thought. It rose, she thought, just like a short phrase in music: tiny crescendo on the double *r*, a matched decrescendo, and then a nice fermata on the final sound.

"How's Marissa doing?"

"Fine," she said.

"I wish I could see her, Ames," her sister said.

"We've a terrible connection," Amy said as her sister's last sentence reverberated like the ancient wailing of mourners. "I'd better hang up."

"You sound a little depressed, Amy. Are you all right?"

"Fine."

"I wish you could come out for a visit."

"Not now," Amy said. "I've got to go now," she added. "Feed the baby."

"No more," Amy said aloud when she had hung up, but Julia's voice had already summoned the memory full force. The hospital scene appeared before her like a pop-up page in a child's book. A clean, well-stocked hospital cafeteria. Wedge-shaped sandwiches, doughnuts, crackers, and cookies are on the counter. Machines are poised, ready to dispense coffee and hot water. Tea bags wait nearby, piled into an empty plastic coffee cup. The serving ladies and their trays of hot macaroni and cheese are absent. Amy moves along the counter, picking up a triangular sandwich and a package of Oreos. She wears slacks and an easy-fitting cotton sweater, clothes selected for comfort through a vigil. The bright lights bother her; she turns from them, closes her eyes, and turns back, but they persist. She had thought the corridors might be dimmed. Wouldn't birth and death be easier in muted lighting? She passes by the coffee, memory warning her that caffeine after nine at night keeps her awake. There is the noise of change at the cash register, and then the terrible scrape of the chair on the floor, and finally a metallic sound, as the legs of the chair and table collide. During the day, she considers, this must not be a problem. There would be many people then, talking. Laughing. Daytime people. The ones who come to see a new baby or a friend with a broken leg. Then the scrape of the chair would be lost in the noise of people. Across the cafeteria, one man sleeps, his head down on the table. Will they come and get him if his person dies?

She bites into her sandwich, and the soft white bread molds itself to her upper palate. She works it off with her tongue, peeling it back carefully, then swallows dutifully: one does not spit things out in public. The Oreos she pushes about like checkers, moving them round and round one another. She does not want the dry chocolate crumbs, like playground dust, cluttering up her mouth. If only her mother hadn't begun to beg for water, if only she weren't lucid. No longer Mama, but now Portrait of a Dying Woman. The artist had failed to capture the subtle combination of anguish and enlightenment usually associated with lingering death. This artist was expert in delineating pain.

Give her water, for Christ's sake.

She'll choke on it. Her reflexes are no longer intact.

Amy has thought about murder. She has thought about bringing water to her mother's lips. For forty-six hours her mother has been begging for water.

Amy piles the cookies into her purse for later, upstairs, when she may grow hungry.

Mama, if I give you the water, you'll choke. You understand, don't you?

And if I tell her I'm pregnant, that there will be a baby she'll never, never see, will that knowledge give her more pain for more losses? How can I tell her now? You ought to have told her weeks ago, Amy.

I ought to have, she thinks. I came to tell her, that same day she told me she was dying. How can I be pregnant when Mama is dying?

We'll name the baby for her, Paul had said.

Upstairs in a patient room, her mother's eyes are closed. Amy hears a new noise, a rattling in her mother's chest, as of bones and lungs and air all mixed improperly. Two nurses hover and the noise increases. Can they get it straightened out? A jump start? A reset button? The rattle fills the room. Amy looks to the walls: to her they appear to vibrate with the sound.

"Is she conscious?" Amy asks.

"No," a nurse answers. Amy sits and watches. Marcy holds her mother's hand. Julia holds Amy's hand. The rattle breaks suddenly from its pattern and resonates at a higher pitch. Hit the automatic reset, Amy thinks, her eyes riveted to a series of buttons on the wall above her mother's head. "Mama," Marcy says. The noise is gone.

Mama, Amy thinks, did you remember that I was only twenty-five? "I should have told her about the baby," she says.

"Ssshhh," Julia says. The three of them have their arms round one another. What is holding me up? Amy wonders, for her feet seem no longer in contact with the floor, but magically to be floating loosely in the air.

"You'll name the baby for her," Marcy says.

"I was her baby," Amy says.

"Ssshh," says Julia.

At the cemetery after the burial, Amy walks beside Rabbi Sampson.

"I don't know about these things," she says.

"Of course not," he says and circles his man's arm around her.

She looks steadfastly down, her feet measuring out the distances between headstones next to the road they walk. Only yesterday, she remembers, she had not been able to feel the earth below her feet, and now she finds it wickedly solid beneath her. Was there a proper way to talk about her pregnancy in the cemetery?

"Paul and I," she says, diluting her own responsibility by including him, "are expecting a baby next winter, but," she adds quickly before he can tell her what joy that knowledge must have

given a dying woman, "she didn't know. It happened too fast."
From the corner of her eye she sees him nod. "I wondered," she
continues, "about naming. Would it be proper, I mean, to name a
baby for her?"

"Of course," he says. "Naming a baby for your mother is a
beautiful way to honor her memory."

"But she was young," Amy protests. "Forty-seven."

"She led a full life. She was a good woman. That's all that
matters. And you give her good name a new life through a child."

"Is it wishing a short life on my child?"

"No," he says. "But come speak to me, you and Paul, if you
like. We can talk together."

"She took a long time to die. And she had so much pain. I
wouldn't want anyone else to have to suffer like that."

"This isn't voodoo, Amy. You may choose to keep her memory
alive through your child, but if it disturbs you, you should give the
child a new name."

Paul has broken away from the group of aunts and uncles and
has started back toward her. The rabbi pats her shoulder. Paul
stands by her now and takes her hand. I can name the baby for her,
she would tell him later. Tell me it's all right if I don't. Of course,
he would say. She would be able to count on that. He had already
said it to her last night while she cried. He had said she didn't have
to ask the rabbi at all. I will not take the first letter of her name,
she thought, and give it to this baby.

She had begun to round out a bit. Just this week she had noticed
it. Just this week while Mama died, she had been unable to bear
the pressure of her pants across her waist. The flesh of her abdomen had begun to itch. The stretching of flesh had begun.

She wouldn't take a single letter of her mother's name. Not one.
There would be no letters in common.

She is thirsty. All day she has been unable to swallow anything,
not even water at breakfast. It'll pass, Paul says. As they drive

through the cemetery gate she remembers another superstition: hold your breath when you pass a graveyard or you will die at midnight. Julia and Marcy thrust handkerchieves at her when she begins to sob.

Twelve

SHE had cut the celery diagonally, as you do for Chinese food. The fragrance of authenticity emanated from the mix of spices.

"If I could get out," she said to Eddie, "I could've gotten to the oriental grocery store downtown. It would have been more authentic that way." She served him his egg fu yung.

"Nothing wrong with this," he said when he had tasted it. "This is the best lunch spot in the Twin Cities, darlin'." She felt the blood rise in her cheeks.

"I'm making lasagna for dinner," she said.

"My favorite," he said. "Wish I could be here." They both laughed.

"Maybe there'll be some left over for lunch tomorrow," she said.

"I'm counting on it," he said. Marissa began to cry. "I'll get her," he said. Eddie was able to eat comfortably with the baby in one arm. He would rock her, and she would stay quiet.

"Why can't I do that?" she asked him.

"She gets reminded of how wonderful nursing is when you hold her."

"Then it's not just experience?" she asked him.

"That helps," he said.

"Lasagna, tomorrow," she said to him when he left.

Amy tucked Marissa under her arm and carried her up the two flights to Mrs. Martin's apartment. She held tight to the railing with the other hand. What if she missed a step? Would she be able to clutch the baby to her body so that she would be protected, or would her own weight end up crushing her still soft skull against the old wooden stairs? Going down was always worse, seeing the whole staircase stretched out below her, and she would have sudden flashes of the baby lying lifeless at the bottom. But it was Thursday, and so she climbed the stairs. Mrs. Martin said that if they had a regular day to visit, they'd both look forward to it all the more. A lingering smell of tuna fish greeted her when Mrs. Martin opened the door.

"I wanted to make Marissa a little afghan," Mrs. Martin explained, and she held up the yards and yards of tangled pink yarn that lay on her chair. "One we might keep here for emergencies, but I lost the end, and now it's hopelessly confused." She was not shaking. She had lifted her glasses onto her forehead while she examined the jumble of knots which flowed over her lap and down round her feet. "I've got a Stilton today," she said.

"I like Stilton," Amy said. Mrs. Martin's stale air had a soporific effect, but Amy didn't mind. She didn't even mind the weekly talk of cheese and knitting. The questions were simple. The answers were simple. Marissa always dozed in the close atmosphere.

"There used to be an old custom, you know," the woman told her, without looking up from her tangles, "that when a girl was ready to marry, the mother of the young man would come to the girl's house with her yarn. Then she'd hand a big confused mess of it, like this one here, and she'd ask the girl to straighten it out. Test her patience, you know. If she could do it, she earned the husband. You have to have a lot of patience to live with a man. To take care of children. So I've always thought that it was a good test, don't you?"

"Yes," Amy said, and she cut the Cheddar into little cubes, the way Mrs. Martin liked to serve it.

"Thank you, dear," she said to Amy. "I'm so caught up with this yarn, I didn't even get to cut the cheeses up nicely. When I finish this," she went on, "I'll have earned my husband, don't you think?"

Amy laughed gently with the old woman, entranced by her fluff of white hair.

"Tell me again what your hubby does."

"He's at the university. He works in an office that handles decisions about university expenditures." She never knew just how much Mrs. Martin understood, nor how much of her nodding was voluntary, how much involuntary. She might have said money, rather than expenditures, she considered.

"He's not a mailman, then?" she asked, her white brows moving together in puzzlement.

"No," Amy said simply and turned Marissa round in her arms, then waited for more. Should she laugh at the woman, Amy wondered, hinting possibly that she was senile? Change the subject, or ask her if she felt all right?

"A friend?" Mrs. Martin pursued.

Amy raised her head slowly, then, with careful deliberation, raised her eyebrows as though very surprised. "Excuse me?" she said.

"The mailman," she said. "Is he your friend?"

"No," Amy said. I must say as little as possible, she told herself.

"Oh," Mrs. Martin said. She dropped her yarn to the floor and began to cut the Stilton. "I'm not being a very good hostess today, getting all wrapped up that way in my yarn." She offered Amy a piece of cheese on a water cracker. "The truck's here so much, I thought he might be a friend."

"I get a lot of packages. Because of the baby, you know. My family all live far away, and they're always sending things." Amy picked up a knife and cut the cubes of Cheddar smaller and smaller. "Sometimes, too, when it's really cold, I make him come in and warm up with cocoa. People do that all the time back East. They don't do it here?" Would cocoa sound more innocent than tea?

"I don't know," she said. "I don't get out much anymore. The world changes quickly nowadays. Not at all like what it used to be."

"Yes," said Amy. She knew she should elaborate as little as possible.

"He stays a while and you talk?" She ran her hand through her white hair.

Amy moved her head up and down in a mechanical nod.

"How nice for both of you," she said. "I know I look forward to your visits. In this weather," she said, "we need to invite others in, don't we?" Amy had a sudden vision of kicking the old woman's chair out from under her and running from the room. Or of standing and telling her, loudly but simply, to go to hell. Instead, she shook Marissa gently while Mrs. Martin gathered up her yarn. The baby whined in protest. "I ought to go," Amy said, rising from her velvet seat. "She needs feeding."

"You don't feed her on demand, do you?"

"No," said Amy, "but she's due now for a feeding and a bath."

"Of course," Mrs. Martin said. "You get along. I thought you might want to help with my tangles. I find it fun, myself, but then, you already have a husband, don't you?" Amy smiled, then turned her glance quickly downward to the dark design of the tablecloth.

"I'll see you next week," Mrs. Martin said, her hands once again plunged deep into her knots. "I'll order another Stilton, then?"

"That'd be lovely," Amy said.

*

In blizzards he was late. And he never stayed long. She sat at the bedroom window, lights out, in her fat sweater, the curtain wrapped round her from behind. There was no one on the street. The wind blew the snow perpendicular to its normal path. It swirled in frenzied cyclones round the shrubs. There was no peace to snow like this. But the whirlwinds were compelling. She could watch them for hours. With blizzards there was the wind. You could hear it all night long.

"This guy at work," Eddie said when she opened the door, "the one who has this letter route, he mouthed off this morning about me parking here. He noticed, Ame."

She tried to picture him, this route man, this mailman who walked from house to house delivering the daily mail, but she could not. Was he black, white? Glasses? Old, young? Had Mrs. Martin called him? Why had she never noticed him? How odd. She'd looked out the window so often for Eddie — had sometimes seen the route man and thought, only very briefly, that it might be Eddie — glanced for the truck and, when it wasn't there, looked away. And he was wrapped, probably, wrapped in the watch cap, the ear muffs, the layers and layers of clothing — jackets and sweaters and sweat shirts.

"The weather's awful," he said. "I can't stay much. Not even lunch, Ame."

"Take your coat off," she said.

"Just a few minutes," he said as he peeled off his jacket. "Should we sit in the kitchen?" he asked when she made no move away from the door.

"If you like," she said.

"Or here?" he asked tentatively, pointing toward the living room.

"If you like," she said.

"Maybe I'll just get going," he said. "It's really bad out there. I think this is the worst snow this year." He tried to see out the windows. "I better go," he said.

"If you like," she said and handed him back his jacket.

The snow did not stop at all that day. Paul called and said he would try to wait till the wind died down before starting back. He would ski home. He sounded exhilarated.

"You sound happy," she said.

"Everybody here thinks this might break the record. We've all got our radios on, so we can hear the latest prediction."

"What record?" she asked him.

"The snowfall record. That's all the radio's talking about. We're not really that close to breaking it, but then, this wasn't supposed to be much of a storm at all, so nobody really knows what's going to happen. It's falling heavily now, and if it keeps up for twenty-four hours, it just might break the record."

"How many more inches till the record?"

"Twenty-three."

She groaned, felt a funny choking in her throat, and hung up the phone. It rang again a few moments later.

"Are you all right?" Paul's voice asked.

"Yes," she said.

"Why did you hang up?"

"I got distracted," she said.

"I just wanted to tell you I might be late. If I wait for the wind, that is."

"It's OK," she said.

"Do you have enough food? Enough milk?"

"Yes."

"There's always the powdered milk, I guess."

"Yes."

"I'll see you as early as I can, but don't wait up, you don't have to."

"OK," she said and hung the phone up once more. She returned to her place at the bedroom window, the drapes encircling her, but she could see nothing at all. Wind had blown the snow over the entire pane. "Joe," she whispered, "Joe." Then even more quietly she said, "She knew he wasn't coming back." It was newborns he liked. Marissa was already getting too old. Too big. That one — where was it — on Ralston? Not a very good neighborhood, really. But it was five pounds. Skinny, helpless. Marissa had changed so much since Eddie had been coming. He had said it — look how chubby she's getting, like a regular Gerber baby, he'd said. Her baby was a girl, that one was a boy. Would it make any difference? "Joe," she whispered again, leaned her forehead on the frigid glass, and cried. She would have thought that because her baby was a girl, it would have made a difference.

Only nine inches of snow fell, not even approaching the record. The snow stopped about midnight, and when Paul returned he kept the radio on in the bedroom, listening over and over again to the announcer bemoaning the Twin Cities' "disappointing failure."

In the morning Amy didn't think she could get out of bed. Her limbs felt heavy and unresponsive. "Is it some kind of flu?" Paul asked. She supposed it was, she said, although she didn't really think so.

"Shall I stay home?" he asked her. "Do you need me to?"

"Need?" she asked him.

"Need. Need me to do things, help with the baby, I don't know."

She didn't know either. What would he do if he stayed home? "I think I can get the baby and nurse her," she said. "That's all I need to do. I won't do anything else."

"What about your own food?" he asked.

"I'm not hungry," she said.

"Shall I come home at lunch?" he asked.

"No," she said.

"What will you eat?"

"I'll eat," she snapped at him.

"I'm trying to be helpful," he said, and Amy waved a hand in front of her face, brushing his words back.

"I've done perfectly all right till now, haven't I?"

He inhaled deeply and turned away. "Can I leave you a sandwich?" he asked in a more natural tone, but still facing away. The notion of conversing this way, to an anonymous back, amused her.

"Maybe jelly," she said without anger.

"Jelly?" he asked, turning, laughing a little.

"It's all I want," she said.

"It's sublimely regressive, Amy."

"It's good when you've got the flu."

He left her sandwich, wrapped in plastic wrap, along with a pitcher of ice water on the night table. "Shall I call you later?"

"No," she said, "I might be asleep."

"I'll bring home takeout," he said. She tried to smile.

"Could you turn on the TV?" she asked as he neared the doorway.

"Sure," he said.

When she had been sick as a child, her mother would lug the kitchen TV up the stairs and put it on top of Amy's bureau. Then they'd snuggle down in the narrow bed together to watch. At lunch time they would have a tea party, with tiny cut-up pieces of toast and real hot tea with honey and water to cool it down. There was an enormous calico bag her mother kept for just such times. If Amy napped, her mother told her, she could reach inside for one of the special things — paper dolls, a coloring book, a puzzle — and when Amy would complain that she wasn't tired enough to sleep, her mother would say, that's wonderful, it shows you're getting better if you're not tired enough to sleep, and then you won't need any more special toys. And so she would try to sleep, would beg her mother to rub her back, to stay right in the bed with her. Pretty soon you'll be too old for all this, her mother would say. But not yet, Amy would protest, I'm not too old yet, am I, and her mother would say, of course not. Amy knew she was in a delicate position — she knew that Marcy, who was only eighteen months older did not get such special treatment. Marcy was too old, and had been for some time. Amy was careful not to jeopardize her situation. She complained very little when she was ill. Didn't demand things, like one more story, please. Said thank you whenever she ought. There were jelly sandwiches and ginger ale and lollipops for dipping into the ginger ale. Pretzels. Arrowroot cookies. Tiny babies eat these, her mother told Amy. They're very easy to digest. That's why I buy them for you when you're sick. So I can be a baby again? she asked. So you can be a baby, her mother said.

"Mama," grown-up, big-sized, malingering Amy said aloud, "I have a baby now." It might have been: her mother would have knocked once on the hospital room door, pushed it open, and walked in. A strong and rumbling hello. There she would be in her good colors, her fine fabrics. Easy wool skirts, reliable Shaker knits. Comfortable, easy: those were her mother's words about how to dress. And she would have picked up the baby. She would have skipped the usual oohs and aahs. What she might have said was, very nice work, baby. Very nice work. Maybe they'd have laughed, the two of them together.

Amy peeled the plastic wrap from the sandwich Paul had made for her and turned it round, checking the edges for extra jelly. Paul was lean on jelly. When her mother had made them, Amy had been able to run her tongue round the edge, gathering all the luscious extra before she even began on the sandwich. In her own house now, she had only grape jelly, kept on hand as accompaniment for Paul's occasional peanut-butter snacks. In her mother's house, there had been mint and apple and plum. Strawberry and raspberry too, sometimes. "You want a jelly sandwich?" her mother used to say. "I'll see if the waitress can get you one."

"Mama," Julia would say, "there's no protein in jelly." And Marcy, younger than Julia, would ask, "Can I get one, too?" But her mother would push both remarks aside and concentrate on her hushed discussion with the waitress. "Is there any way," she would whisper conspiratorially, "that we could get a jelly sandwich for the little one? She's very allergic to everything. I wouldn't want to take a chance."

Amy finished her jelly sandwich, wished there were ginger ale instead of water, and wondered if you could still buy arrowroot cookies in the supermarket.

Amy discovered something lovely that morning: the baby liked to sleep on her chest. Marissa snuggled down on Amy's chest just as though she were nesting, and fell fast asleep. Then Amy fell asleep, too, and woke only when Marissa began to squirm and stretch above her. Captain Kangaroo and Mr. Moose were laughing raucously on the screen. Carrying the baby with her, she entered her drapery hideaway to view the final results of the blizzard. The drift that had blocked her view the day before had been partially blown away again. The sun was surprisingly strong, compensating for its culpable absence the day before. Marissa cried in her arms. Distractedly, Amy touched a finger to the infant's lips, and she quieted. Lips sucked finger noisily. A flurry of dry snow flew by, projected from the shovel of the next-door neighbor. The scrape of metal on concrete, the muffled whirr of snowblowers reassured: they were digging out. The sounds of heavy chains on vehicles told her the streets were passable. He might come today, after all. His peculiar visit yesterday might be explained so easily: there had been a blizzard. How foolish her behavior of the last twenty-four hours now seemed. He would be back. The route man, Mrs. Martin, they wouldn't keep him away. He wouldn't let them bother him.

And was it possible she was getting used to this winter, after all? She felt quite light-headed this morning, seeing that sunshine, hearing those snow shovels. How lovely it would be to take a baby for a stroll. It couldn't really be done, of course, not with all the snow on the sidewalks. Even shoveling might be invigorating. It'd probably tire her, but the cold might feel bearable if she were exercising like that. She breathed deeply, imagining the cold air exchange. Paul would surely have done the front walk before he left, but there would be the back, still. Where would she leave Marissa while she shoveled? Couldn't really leave her alone in the house, could she? She would compromise and do the only really practical thing under the circumstances — she would open all the shades and draperies as absolutely far as she could and let in the sun as much as possible, and it might reduce some of the ice. Then, she would call the grocery and proceed with lunch, just as she always did. She wouldn't give in. She had been depressed yesterday, that was all, believing the worst of him because he'd run off so fast. But she wouldn't be depressed anymore. In fact, she would make something special, she thought. It would have been completely understandable if he hadn't even come at all in a blizzard. At least he had stopped by. "Joe," she said aloud, "you get yourself over here, cause I wanna see you." That was telling him, she thought and smiled. And she'd bake cookies to celebrate his return.

"I was almost afraid to come today," he announced as he stepped into the hallway. She kissed him suddenly, lightly, on the mouth. It made her even more light-headed than before. "Why?" she asked him.

"You seemed angry at me yesterday."

"I wasn't angry," she said.

"You're sure?" he asked. She nodded. "I thought of calling, but then I thought I better not."

"I'm glad you came," she said. "If you hadn't come, who'd have eaten my chocolate chip cookies?" The phone rang, and she left him still struggling with his boots. "I'm much better," she said into the phone. "I slept a few extra hours, and I feel completely recovered."

"Good," Paul said. "I was worried."

"You just felt guilty," she said.

"Perhaps. In any case, I'm glad you're feeling better. I'll see you later."

"Was that Paul?" Eddie asked when she had replaced the receiver.

"Yes," she said.

"Weren't you feeling well or something?"

"No, I thought I might have the flu, but it was something more transient. I'm fine now."

Eddie lifted the sleeping Marissa from her carriage. The infant's eyes opened briefly, but he rocked her back to sleep. "Does he know I come for lunch?"

"No." She stopped at the sink, the water running, the kettle swinging in her hand.

"Do you think about telling him?"

"No," she said and broke the steady stream of water by moving her finger back and forth through it.

"Do you lie about it?"

"It doesn't come up, I guess."

"If it came up, if he said, who ate the rest of the meat loaf or something, what would you do?" He took the kettle from her hand and filled it.

"I think I'd lie."

"What would he do if he knew?"

"I'm not sure. He might act pleased at first. He might say he was glad I had company. If I didn't tell him you were better with Marissa than he is, he might not mind."

"She's his first baby. She's my sixth."

She smiled at him. "Joe," she said, "you're the funniest man I know."

"Are you going to tell him?"

What could she say to Paul? The mailman comes in for lunch? Joe brings me linzer tortes and bathes Marissa? He laughs and rocks her to sleep? "No," she said. "Do you think I should?"

"I don't know," he said. "I suddenly started thinking about it when I thought you were angry at me. I thought, maybe it isn't anger, maybe her husband is suspicious, or knows, or something."

"We're not lovers," she said, then added, when he had moved his black eyebrows inquisitively, "you and I, I mean."

"No," he said, looking away from her, down toward the sleeping infant. Will we be lovers? she wondered. What were the necessary prerequisites for such an arrangement? Here was the conversation she wished she could have with him: Might we be lovers or are we trying to be lovers or even wanting to be lovers? Do you think of the word for us at all? Do you think of it constantly? Desperately? Aren't we lovers now? Wasn't I wrong, didn't I misspeak? If you have thought about us being lovers, and I have thought about us being lovers, and if someday we become lovers, doesn't that mean we are really lovers now, but simply at the beginning of a long continuum of loving? If we both think about it and we don't become lovers, does that change what we are now? What if we can't be lovers, anymore than I can be a lover to Paul? I have thought: Will we be lovers? but nothing else. Not even ought we to be lovers? Marissa cried and he renewed his rocking. Amy looked toward the spot on the kitchen floor where the sun had burned so invitingly as she baked the cookies. It was gone. Through the window over the sink she could see that the sky had lost its blue, returned to its accustomed wet grey. "O metaphor," she said aloud and laughed. He lifted his head and smiled directly at her.

"What do you suppose we are, then?" he asked.

"What do you mean?"

"If we're not lovers?"

"Friends?" she asked.

"Friends," he whispered, reached one hand behind her head and stroked her hair. "Good friends," he whispered and kissed her mouth.

"Joe," she whispered.

"You're the funniest woman I know," he said.

"Is it a secret from your wife?" He extended his open hand to her, and she placed her own hand upon his.

"It's a secret, but it won't be one for long if I come every day. I can't come every day, Ame, can you understand that?"

"How often?"

"Twice a week."

"Three times?" she asked.

"I shouldn't come at all, Ame."

"Twice, then."

"When the spring comes, you need to start taking this bundle outside, getting her used to the world."

"Spring won't come." Kisses. And lovers where? In that bed of Paul's? Who are you, Joe? A spirit that creeps into the bedroom at night, or the fairy godmother who rocks my baby to sleep? Will you give her gowns and coaches of gold, Joe? Or will you give me those kisses?

"Spring'll come. The baby's getting big. You don't need to hang around here so much, I don't think. I'm slowing you down now. I'm not helpful anymore."

"You are, Eddie."

"Well, no more than twice a week, anyway, OK? And when there's a package."

"Eddie," she pleaded.

"I can't, Ame. I'm sorry." In fairy tales, she pondered, the magic powers never lasted, did they? They came and set the old shoemaker and his wife on their feet again, grew a beanstalk just long enough for Jack to get treasures, and gave Cinderella the wherewithal to get together with the prince, but then, after that, they were all on their own. Squander the treasures or displease the prince, and it's back to poverty and injustice again. If you leave, Joe, I can't do it myself.

"What's for lunch?" he asked.

"Sandwich steaks."

"Hard rolls?" he asked.

"Of course."

When he had gone, she wrote in her notebook: "Lovers?"

Thirteen

$\mathcal{B}$ACK in his truck, Eddie watched his own hand shaking on the gearshift lever. He moved it back and forth, back and forth between the gears. "I should get out," he said aloud. "I should get out before it's too damn late." He forced the lever to the upper left and eased out the clutch. The truck lurched unpleasantly over a frozen patch, then hopped partway down the street before it smoothed out.

By that evening he had worked out a plan. Deena sat next to him on the couch, and three of the kids lay sprawled in front of them watching TV. He turned the fruit bowl round and round on the coffee table, then pulled out two apples and began shining them with a cloth napkin. He would wait three days, he thought, come back late (late for the pattern they'd gotten into recently, maybe about twelve-thirty) and say he'd have just a cup of tea, and tell her he'd come only if there were packages. She would try to bargain for more, he knew. If there were a way to do it without having to show up again, it would be easier in some ways, but he couldn't do that to her. He would explain to her that he'd suddenly realized — what? He couldn't say — but here he stumbled badly in his thinking, for he didn't even want to phrase the words in his head. Didn't want to allow that he might say them. Might mean them. He could just give an excuse, any excuse, really, just so she knew he wouldn't be there, just so she wouldn't wait for him all the time. I can't come anymore because I got called on the carpet by my boss. She would look at him silently (what people called a blank stare — although it cut right through him, so it couldn't be blank, could it?), and then she'd look away, as though she'd lost interest.

The word *lovers* had started him feeling panicky. Like you feel when you jump into freezing water and the breath gets knocked clear out of you. We're not lovers, she had said, as though she was correcting him. But if it was really nervousness he felt, why had he kissed her? Why then? She kissed with a softness that made him want to cry. All soft, yet there was a kind of blankness in her kiss as in her stare: no implications, no tomorrow. How much older was he? Ten years, maybe? He could have said — and he could almost feel her wrist now in his hand, almost wrap his fingers round hers — he could have said, should we be lovers? They'd still see each other when there was a delivery. There were fewer now. Eventually they'd stop. Like a natural dying-out process. Less and less often, then it would be all over. Three days would be Friday. He knew that planning what you were going to say to someone wasn't necessarily a good idea. It was better to just see what happened Friday. He finished shining the Red Delicious apples and handed one to Deena. This is my wife, he thought. And in here, in this room, in this house, is my life. If he were to keep thinking that, he would have the strength to do it, he was sure. This is my wife, he repeated to himself, this is my life.

On Wednesday morning there was a package for Amy. See, he told himself, what good is planning? Now he couldn't stay away till Friday — it would actually be a violation of law. He had no choice but to deliver her parcel. Once he had thought: I could have two lives. Deena need never know. Amy's husband need never know, and it seemed like they might be thinking of separating, anyway. I belong here, he had thought, as he pulled the truck in front of her house, as much as I belong in my own home. He would tell her.

But which would he tell her? That he belonged or that he didn't belong? I'll try, he said, very much aloud, as he waited for her to answer his ring.

The package was from her sister. "Bless that woman," she said when she read the address.

"I was thinking the same thing," he said.

"I didn't think you'd come today," she said as she arranged his jacket on the doorknob, "so we'll have a kind of potluck lunch, if you don't mind."

"Of course not."

"You could bathe her today," Amy said.

"Maybe I shouldn't," he said as they sat down together at the table.

"Why not?"

"You can do it now. It doesn't scare you anymore, does it?"

"No. I like her splashes, and afterwards she always nurses well. She drinks without stopping and drains all my milk." She had her arms crossed over her breasts, almost, he thought, as though she were hugging herself. "She's not like that at her other feedings," Amy continued. "She's more distracted, I guess, more picky or something. But you like to bathe her, don't you?" He nodded. "You can."

"Not today," he said. "I'll leave it for you."

"It's really the nursing that I like," she said, "and I'll still have that."

"I just want you to get used to doing it without me."

"Eddie," she said, kind of low and gravelly the way she sometimes did, "I can do it myself. But I can also share it with you. I'll share it all if you like."

There were other things he thought about saying, with words like *realistic* and *slowing down* in them, but they were just bits and pieces of what he ought to say, not enough to make sense. If he could tie it together and just say it outright once, "I'm not coming back anymore," it would be done. Would she cry? He mustn't consider that but just try to say it, and then he heard the broken awkwardness of his own voice as he said, "I won't be coming anymore," and he thought of his youngest when she cried because the peanut butter made her tongue stick to the roof of her mouth.

"Nonsense," she said.

"Except for the packages," again, unevenly.

"Not yet," she said quietly. "I still need you." She reached for his hand. "A little longer, Joe, please." She brought his hand to her mouth and kissed it. He covered her mouth with his hand, and she closed her eyes and kissed his palm over and over. "With a new baby, with this weather, Joe, . . ." he stroked her hair. Did it make a difference? In the long run, did it make a difference? How would the courts view it? The prosecution would claim lust, the defense would paint him as the Good Samaritan. He would be called to the stand. He would break under the cross-examination. He would raise his arms — a plea for mercy from the gods. He would turn his eyes upward and confess, "I am everything you say I am," then clutch the rail in front of him, and watch while Deena sobbed quietly into a handkerchief.

"When the weather breaks," he said, "I leave, OK?"

"Just as long as you come sometimes now." The baby had begun to cry.

"Maybe I will bathe her," he said. "Then you can get lunch ready."

When they'd all been fed, she slid the string from her package and ripped the brown paper from the box. "Pajamas for me," she said as she lifted the flannel contents of the box out for him to examine. "With feet," she said, and they both laughed. "Look," she said, "the feet come off. But I'm not taking them off. I freeze at night. I curl up tight as can be to try to keep warm."

He thought of two people in a double bed. If they didn't warm one another, there wasn't much room to be separate. There might even be danger of them falling off the sides of the bed. No one warms you? Perhaps they had a larger bed, and he hadn't realized it, a queen, a king. He would look later. "Cute pajamas," he said. "Cute birds," and he pointed to the repeated design of red birds in flight against the pink flannel.

"She says if these fit, she can send more." Amy held a letter in her hand.

"What's it like out there, in Maryland?" he asked.

"You mean the weather?"

"Yeah."

"Right now it's not terrific. February's a bit grey. We even get some snow, usually in February. A few inches, maybe, and it sometimes turns to ice if the temperature goes up and down. It's damp, too. But the buds have begun by March first. The crocuses are up. Then the forsythia comes. End of March the daffodils sometimes have started. The grass is green in April. I suppose you don't see grass here till nearly June."

"Real bad snow years, maybe. Sometimes in those really bad years there'll be some snow on the ground still in May."

"And Eddie, on weekends we would get in the car and go to the Shenandoah Valley in Virginia. Summer in April, there, Eddie, and so much green you could burst. You can lie in the grass and feel the sun strong on your face in March."

He took her hand. "No trouble keeping warm at night?" he asked.

"None," she said. "You sleep without pajamas. You don't have to pull the blankets up round your neck." In June we can do that here, he thought. "Were you here in June?"

"We came in August. August 14th. It was hot. Hot, hot, hot.

Then one day it cooled off. Summer into winter. I suppose it goes the same way from winter into summer."

"Some years." He watched her stretch back in her chair, her arms extended way above her head, the cotton of her full red shirt waving gently round her. "Why'd you two come out here?" he asked.

She sat back up and looked off toward the window. "Silliness," she said.

"Silliness?"

"We wanted to do something different. We'd been in New Haven forever. Paul had been a graduate student there and we'd never gotten around to leaving. We both had good jobs, but we always thought of the whole arrangement as temporary. Someday we would go to some new exciting place. Then one day we just decided the time had come. After we'd been here a month, I said to myself, OK, now I've seen Minnesota. That's nice. Now I'd like to see California and Texas and Colorado and Arizona and Mississippi. And then the snow came, and I really knew I didn't want to stay."

"Why didn't you go to Maryland instead of here?"

"Partly because it was too tame. We'd both grown up there. And my mother was dead, so I didn't feel as though I had a real hometown anymore. I liked the idea of having a new starting place, a new town to be from. So Paul and I started thinking of all sorts of other crazy places to live. It was a nice game, imagining all those cities and towns."

He slipped his hand along her arm, the full sleeves of her shirt draping softly round his hand. "Did your mother die recently?"

"Last spring. The rhododendron and laurel were out in her backyard. We sat on lawn chairs out there while my uncle — he was her attorney — read the will. My aunt made iced tea. She took charge. She made the funeral arrangements. My uncle urged us to sell the house. Talking about wood-frame structures and market values seemed offensive to me, but I didn't know what else to do. Each night while it was on the market, I'd lie in bed saying, Mama, I'm sorry. And I'd call the agent in the morning and say it had to be nice people who bought it, she had to be sure they were nice. It sold quickly. Then we didn't know what to do with the contents. My aunts and uncles didn't seem to want to be involved anymore; they seemed distracted. I think my aunts were beginning to worry about cancer, about their own health. Every time I looked at my Aunt Anna, she was touching her breasts, checking for lumps. The real estate agent suggested an estate sale. It sounded clean and neat, so we did it." Her grip on his arm was firm. "She wasn't fifty yet."

"And your father?" he asked.

"He died when I was six." She released his arm, then held out her hand, palm up as if in supplication, and he entwined his fingers with hers. "Paul and I went down to visit her three weeks before she died. We arrived early. She hadn't finished cleaning. She had her shoes off, and she had climbed up on the dining room table to chase away a cobweb she'd seen on the chandelier. I knew something was wrong. She was aged suddenly. I said, 'Mama, are you sick?' and she sat down right on the table and cried. Julia was there. She knew. So did Marcy, because they lived so close by. They hadn't told me. Didn't want me to worry. I'm the baby sister."

"Family secrets are the worst kind," he said.

"We took some things: the fine things, the things that my mother especially liked and kept out all the time. I left my share with my sisters. Except for my blue cookie plate. I took that. I'll get the rest someday, I suppose. Julia was supposed to do the kitchen. I watched her walk through the kitchen and open every drawer and close it without taking anything out. I don't think she saw what was in any of them. Marcy's husband carried the silverware out the front door, and I went through the jewelry. I put it in three bags and handed it out, like loot at a grade-school party. It seemed like stealing, Eddie, because she should have been entitled to twenty-five more years' use out of everything. Then Marcy and I went to the sale. The liquidator wanted someone from the family to be there so that afterwards we wouldn't claim that he violated our instructions. He had put price tags on everything in the house. On her underwear, her one-cup measurers, her magazines and notebooks. People were pulling open the drawers and clawing through their contents. Then they stood in line in the living room and paid their quarters and dimes. Marcy and I went out and sat on the back stairs and cried. I don't know why we didn't take the things ourselves. Estate sales are for people without descendents. We were unkind."

"But she was dead, Ame."

"I know that. But people looked in her books, looked in her closets. I kept seeing images of her barricading closet doors with her dying body."

"What about Paul?"

"What do you mean?"

"Where was he during all of this? Was he there?"

"For some of it. He came to the funeral, but then he went back to New Haven for a while. I needed to make the decisions."

Who was Paul in her life, anyway? Did she care? Did he? If you're not together in a crisis, when are you? "I see why you wanted to go far away," he said.

"Marissa has no one here. Out there she would have had cousins and aunts and uncles. And Paul's parents. Her grandparents."

"You have no one here, either."

"If we'd gone to Virginia, I think that would have been fine. We wouldn't have been that close to where I grew up. There would be memories, but I think I could have lived with that."

"We wouldn't have met," he said gently. She squeezed his hand.

"Joe," she said, "you should come back with me. I want to start over." It's too late, my darlin', he thought. Too late for more silliness. I have a wife. "You should see the Blue Ridge Mountains. Their colors shimmer in the spring sunshine. All blue green. I wish you could see it. Would you miss snow, do you think, if you left?"

"I might. We're all winter people here, I guess. Marissa will be if she stays."

"I guess she'll stay, and we'll be here forever. Besides, the next place we choose might be even worse."

"Why do you make it sound so final? You two might have made a mistake. You might have to face up to that."

"I think Paul's risen to the challenge. I think he wants to stay." Eddie stood up, a sleeping baby tucked under his arm. "I've got to go, Ame."

"Come back soon, Eddie?"

"Soon, darlin'," he said as he rocked the baby back down to her resting place. She did not wake. "Why don't you go back for a visit?" he asked her.

"I'd never come back," she laughed.

"How long you think it'd take to drive?"

"Two days, maybe."

"That's not really too bad."

"Take two weeks off, Joe, and we can do it nice and slow." He put his hands on her shoulders and kissed her.

"Sounds real nice, darlin'. Unrealistic, but very nice."

"Joe, you won't believe what spring is like in those mountains." He kissed her again.

A disturbing dream for Eddie. He stood in the middle of a kitchen — her kitchen — arms in the air like a captured suspect. He was sweating in the dream, praying that the gun aimed at the small of his back wasn't loaded. (Would someone really aim at the small of the back, he later wondered, or would they aim higher, trying for the heart or brain?) Then in the dream he had nerved himself, turned, and found Amy sitting at the table, plates of brownies all around her. She was wiping her mouth with a napkin and smiling.

Then he had fallen to his knees and wept. He must have sobbed out loud or made some noise, for he was startled awake by his wife's hand moving across his chest, and her voice, soothingly saying, "Eddie, honey, what's wrong?" He felt his rapid heartbeat pounding against Deena's hand.

"A dream," he said.

"Tell me," she said, and she kissed his bare chest.

"I can't remember," he said. "You know how they are. You just remember they're scary. I think I was dying."

"Were you falling?"

"I think so."

"You didn't hit bottom, did you?"

"No."

"It means you died, you know, if you do. Really died." She sat up next to him. "Do you want to make love?" she asked him. She combed her fingers through his hair.

"I don't think I can," he said.

She slid back under the covers. "Can you fall back to sleep?" she asked him.

"I think so," he said. It truly surprised him when he couldn't. He turned from side to side, but each time he placed his head on the pillow, he would see Amy, looming in front of him, larger and darker than she really was. He inhaled deeply, slowly, for he had heard that could help you to relax. He turned to his other side and thought he caught the scent of her black hair. He turned again and saw the outline of her breasts under the soft folds of her blouse. Breasts full and growing even larger as they filled with milk. Face into the pillow now, he saw his own children in a line, in order of size, and he tried to explain things to them. The two youngest cried, the second oldest walked out of the room, and the oldest said, "You're sick, you know that? You're sick." Who would understand? Paul Gold? He wanted to be able to say to all of them, I remember about having babies. I remember when Deena locked herself in her room, afraid to come out, afraid to touch Elizabeth because she thought she'd do something horrible to her. "She cried and cried while I made the casserole," Deena had sobbed out to him, "and I thought about putting her in the pot and closing the lid. I heard her flesh sear when I thought it," she said in frantic little gasps. She had grown quiet then and said, almost in a whisper, "and other times, Eddie, I've thought about throwing her down the cellar stairs." His first impulse had been to grab the baby and run out the door. But he had calmed his own breathing and begged her to open the door. He would come home earlier. He would make the dinners. He had rubbed her back and told her the evil feelings would go away. She had been twenty. Only a few years older than Elizabeth, that same baby, was now. Too young.

He had taken the oversized casserole to the basement and stuck it away on a shelf, but it had tormented him even from down there under the floorboards. Eventually he had thrown it into the car and taken it over to the Salvation Army. "It was a wedding gift," Deena had said to him. "Practically brand new."

"You're a real jerk, Dad," he heard the eldest, that same baby, say. What should I have done for Amy? Called her husband at work and urged him to take a few afternoons off a week in order to be home with her? Recommended counseling?

The next night the dream began again. He stood with his arms raised over his head, walking through her apartment. This time some part of his psyche was outside the dream and warned him to wake up. He sat up, wide awake, before the weeping part of the dream. She had worn that dark maroon–colored Indian shirt. The full soft one. And the huge sweater she sometimes wore, that he thought about wrapping round her and then unwrapping like a blanket round a baby. Deena slept beside him. He flipped onto his stomach and put his face into the pillow. He focused carefully on the interiors of Italian restaurants. There was a lot of variety among them, he thought. Adolfo's had those stucco-like walls and live plants hanging all about. But so much more money that Guido's, with its dinette-type chairs. Adolfo's had booths. And the cheaper places were mostly just lasagna. You could get a fine, creamy lasagna, it was true, at Guido's, but if you wanted seafood (and Deena loved seafood), forget Guido's. Unless you just wanted shrimp scampi. Guido's did a very nice scampi. In fact, they did it as well as Adolfo's and really gave you a bigger portion for less. Adolfo's preparation was more attractive — twisted lemon slices, perfectly arranged flat-leaf parsley. And, now that he considered it, the sauce was lighter, more subtle. You didn't get completely knocked out by the garlic. And no other restaurant in the Twin Cities, except Adolfo's, did stuffed calamari. If you wanted it, you made up your mind to pay the difference. It was more elegant, there was no doubt. He fell asleep when they brought the scungilli cocktail.

"I had another dream last night," he told her over Adolfo's tortellini in brodo. He clutched his spoon so tightly, his joints ached.

"A dying dream?" she asked.

"No. This one was different."

"Don't they do nice soups here, Ed?" He nodded. "So what was this dream about?"

"I dreamt I was having an affair," he said, then added quickly, "did you ever have a dream like that?"

"Yes," she said, and he thought she blushed, although it was difficult to tell in the dimly lit room.

"Who was the man?"

"I don't know." She gestured with her spoon, as though in dismissal, and scattered some soup onto the tablecloth. Her hand brushed awkwardly at the wet spots.

"It doesn't matter," he said, and he covered her hand with his. "Who did you dream about in these dreams?"

"No one I really knew. Made-up people, I guess. But they were usually young, I think."

"Boys, you mean?"

"Not that young. Twenties, maybe. They're always different men and different situations, but they're always very intense." She paused and then whispered, "Sexually intense, I mean."

"Do you make love in the dreams?" he asked.

"I don't think so. I think we're always just about to, but the anticipation is always killing."

"Do you think we don't make love enough?"

"I don't think it's that," she said in a barely audible whisper. "I mostly have the dreams on nights we've made love."

"Have you," he said, then paused, considering for a moment the merits of continuing, "ever done it with anyone else?"

"You know I haven't," she said in a sharp whisper.

He nodded solemnly. "Why not?"

"Eddie, cut it out."

"Seriously, why not?"

"Are you telling me you think I should have an affair?"

"No."

"Maybe you're having one." She giggled, then stopped and looked directly at him.

"No," he said. "I was just making high-class Italian restaurant conversation. Don't get upset now, OK?" She nodded. "All right, so why have you never had an affair?"

"I don't want to have an affair. We're married. You'd kill me, anyway, wouldn't you?"

"I don't know. I'd be angry. But you could keep it a secret, don't you think?"

"I don't think so," she said after a pause. "I'd keep thinking you knew. Then I'd probably just tell you. But I'm not going to have an affair. What are you worried about?"

"I'm not worried. I love you. I wanted to know if you love me."

"I love you." They entwined their hands now, and the waiter, arriving to clear their soup plates, stepped back and moved on to another table for a time. "But I wouldn't know how to begin an affair, anyway. I don't know anybody, for one thing. There isn't anybody who's a good prospect, you know what I mean?"

"How about your girl friend Andrea's husband?"

"Eddie, that's obscene."

"Why?"

"He's married. To Andrea. That's a bad example."

"OK, then, imagine somebody accidentally came along. Somebody who was available."

"With us still together?"

"Of course."

"No. I'm too old. Too set. I like it the way it is. We've been married seventeen years." She lowered her head and whispered to him, "I'm too old to risk taking my clothes off for somebody else." He laughed quietly and kissed her mouth. Another reason why he thought Adolfo's was worth the difference in price: you could sit next to each other in a booth.

"You're beautiful, darlin', and I don't want you taking your clothes off for anybody else, you hear? That's my body you've got under those clothes, understand?" He stroked her shoulder and neck. "You understand, don't you?" he asked and kissed her once more.

"Yes," she whispered.

When the cheesecake arrived, she asked him, "Have you ever had an affair?"

"No," he said. "Only dreams."

Fourteen

"Look," Eddie said, "if you visit your sisters, it'll take your mind off other things. And you can get a little sun and springtime under your belt." She did not react. "When you come back," he said, "you'll be refreshed. You can start over." He was finding it harder to continue. His voice felt raspy to him, like a bad sore throat that had come on suddenly. He put his hand to his throat. "We can both start over," he said. She might not have heard, he had said it so low and quiet. "It'll be like I disappeared. We'll start our other lives again." He had hoped she would react. He wondered if he ought to look stern, as though he demanded an answer. "What do you think?" he said, not at all sternly. They were sitting face to face, but she only looked back, peaceful, breathing slow and even, and he had looked down at the alternating pattern of their legs. My leg, her leg, my leg, her leg, between, next, not touching, but almost touching, knee to thigh, thigh to knee, and later he knew, it was absolutely his fault, his fault. He had closed his legs round hers, and somehow they had just folded up together, with kisses that pulled everything out of him, and her little noise, and oh Christ he was doomed. She had told him she couldn't make love, was afraid it wouldn't work, that it hadn't worked with Paul. It's all right, he'd said, and meant it. They lay on the bed and held each other till Marissa cried and Amy got her and brought her back to the bed and nursed her, her shirt all undone. He told her how sad it made him, though, that all his babies were bottle-fed.

"That other baby," she said as she buttoned her shirt. "The one on Ralston."

"What?" he asked. That tiny little premie he'd seen?

"Do you love her, too?"

"The mother?" he said.

She nodded, like a judgement, like she already condemned him for infidelity, he thought. "Ame," he said, "I always figured any mailman who went into houses was getting laid. They always wanted everyone to think so, anyway. I never went into a house, except one. That was an old woman's house. I used to carry her garbage out on Mondays and bring the cans back Tuesdays. She's been dead four years. It was when I had a daily route. I never went in that house on Ralston."

"Why here, then?"

He shook his head. "You asked me . . ."

"All you need is asking? No one else ever asked?"

"It was you. You carrying round that weight that turned out to be Marissa. You were lost-looking."

She made a face at him.

He should not have put it that way, he thought. "Your smile lit things up," he said to her, and he hoped she didn't think he was just being corny and sappy. She had a little flash of a smile that would come up sometimes. He had seen it right from the begin- ning, when he was still standing in the snow. It had drawn him. It wasn't a lie. It wasn't an exaggeration. "But the asking was important," he said to her. "I wouldn't be here if you hadn't asked." He kissed her mouth and then kissed the baby, who still rested in her lap.

At the door she said to him, "What will we do now?" She gave him his sandwich to eat in the truck.

He shrugged. "You'll go away," he said.

She put her arms around him, round the damp wet snow clothes. "We'll talk more," she said.

"Sure," he said. "We'll have to talk again." Doomed, he thought. I'm a goddamned foolish bastard, is all.

He thought of it this way: for me it wouldn't be so bad. I've been married seventeen years. No matter what Deena might think initially, she wouldn't go off after seventeen years. For Paul it would be different. There had not been enough years between them, he thought, to lock them together. The infidelity had long ago been committed, as far as he was concerned. That they met so often, shared so much, and could not stop meeting was their sin. And had it changed either marriage? Not his, he didn't think. And hers? How could he tell? They might not have lasted, postman or no postman.

Would putting his cock into her change things? Why was that so very different from touching her hair? Making her lemonade? The evil man, leading her, stubbornly, steadfastly, astray. He would wake in the night, rock-hard, thinking of her. In his truck, now, he felt the intense heat that he had come to identify with thoughts of her sweep over him. He wondered if they were to make love whether he would at least be less consumed by the idea. The unknown would be known, and the anticipation would be gone. It was the anticipation, wasn't it, that was killing? Why should he expect that sleeping with Amy would be different from sleeping with Deena? Why did it drive him mad like this? Was it simply because it was forbidden and as yet undone? If they were to make love, he might be able to think again. And then, she, too, could get back to living.

*

They made love while Marissa slept. Amy had no pain.

She hadn't expected his chest to be hairless. That smoothness made him seem very young. Like a kid in day camp, she thought, shirt off, swinging his baseball bat, and carefully cracking the brim of his blue cap. Arching that brim just enough, not too much. He sat naked on her sheets, his knees pulled up, arranging her dark hair in patterns on the pillow. That too, made him seem young, that way of sitting, curled up like an adolescent. He had covered her with a blanket. She was glad: her oversized breasts seemed out of place with his spare body.

She had lain awake the night before imagining that which was to come. I have but to ask, she knew. She dreamt of him. A dream unlike dreams she'd had before. She would wake and return to the dream. Marissa cried, but she would not go to her. Paul crawled from the bed, and Amy returned to her dream. She controlled it, said, start over, more, let me see it again, and she did. She got to see the kissing, the undressing, heard her own passionate weeping as he touched each part of her body, all of it, over and over again. She felt the heat of his come, the warmth of her milk as it flowed over both their bodies. The dream was so intense, she felt certain Paul would see it too. It seemed to be all over the bed, leaping up from the pillows into her consciousness. Into anyone's consciousness, entirely unbidden, she feared. In the morning, she thought she could see it on the sheets. She stripped the bed as soon as she and Paul rose.

When it happened, the quietness of their lovemaking had seemed unreal. As a lover, he made her think of a Tai Chi expert she had once seen, stylized and rhythmical. She, the watcher, was hypnotized by the dance. She saw his buttocks, smooth, too, like his chest, contract and release with his strivings. She admired his buttocks, as she admired the rest of his body, for its simplicity. Its only decoration was the jet black hair framing his genitals. She had watched him moving in and out of her body, gathering his speed, and had heard his moan, floating into the room like the distant echo of the vanquished. She saw him in his moment of orgasm reach and strain. But where was the heat of his semen? Why didn't she feel it? She tried listening for it, the explosion of his being in hers, but she heard nothing. He was not heavy as he lay on her. She touched her own nipples: they were dry.

He wanted the window open afterwards, and she begged him not to, said she was afraid. Afraid they would be seen, but he convinced her, closed the curtains in front of the window, and, together, they watched the curtains billowing out toward them, sending out icy breezes that drove them back under the covers. "I love it," he said as he stood, arms outstretched before the shielded window just before he closed it. She laughed. She liked it, too.

She reached under his jacket, pulling herself toward him as he prepared to go. Now he would disappear. "You're not Joe when you're not here, are you?" she asked him. "No," he said. "I'm Eddie Stevens." She had heard his name at last. She knew who he was when he was elsewhere. A slew of nasty curses on his other life slipped through her mind, and she sighed, glad they had not stayed long enough to realize utterance.

She lay down again on the bed. We'll go East now, she thought. The suitcases were right under the bed. Right beneath them when they had made love. "Joe," she said, "our suitcases."

Now we own one another, he thought. I have reached inside her and have seen everything there is to see. There is no part of her hidden, anymore. I am at the center of her.

They had made love, and she had looked at him with that surprised look, again, as if to say, who are you, or what are you doing here? He had asked her, does it hurt? And she had said not at all.

Why had she not been able to do it with Paul? Why did it seem, as he tried to remember it, that he had been holding his breath the whole time? That she, too, had held her breath? He felt his blood pulsing along his inner thighs. He heard the echoes of that throbbing all around him. What now? he wondered. Home again, home again, jiggity jog? I don't look different, he thought. Deena would see nothing different. Nothing at all.

His youngest met him as he pulled in the driveway. She had a snowman to show him. They scuffled briefly with snowballs. "Daddy," said his ten-year-old while he took off his boots, "will you play Monopoly?"

"In a little while, maybe," he said. "Let me talk to Mama first."

"Promise?" she said.

"OK," he said, and he ran his hand over her short, cropped hair. She took his boots from him and lined them up with the others on a mat in the hallway. She ran toward the stairs. "See you later, and don't you forget, or I'll kill you," she shouted.

"Shhh," he admonished. "I won't forget." He saw Deena peeling potatoes at the sink.

"Hello, Love," she said, turning briefly toward him, then back to her task. "Are you tired?" she asked him. He walked to the sink and stood next to her.

"A little," he said. She wiped her hands on a dish towel and put her arms round his neck. He felt her hipbone against his own, her thighs against his own, and he kissed her. He loved them both.

"Do you need help?" he asked.

"Not really," she said, "it's an easy dinner. The girls set the table already. You can go sit down for a while."

"Daddy," the Monopoly voice called down the stairs.

"Fifteen minutes, Josie," he said. "You've got to let me sit down first for a few minutes."

"I'll set the timer," she shouted, as she bounced back down the stairs.

"No," he said. "No bells or alarms. Just tell me when fifteen minutes is up."

"OK," she said, kicking each stair as she climbed.

He sank down into his oversized club chair. So it was done. Was he more bigamist or adulterer? Lunch with one wife, dinner with another. Deena would leave him no matter what he called it, if she were to find out. Saying, "I love her, Deena," would not help. He did love Amy, though. And he loved the baby. Marissa's birth was still there in the fullness of Amy's breasts and the roundness of her hips. While he was in her, he had thought about making another baby with her. Crazy thoughts. And now that they were lovers, he supposed he would only become crazier. He was a fool to have thought it would be different. He had conned himself, of course, talking himself into thinking sleeping with her would free him. He rested his face in his hand. And there would be no choosing, no deciding on options, once Deena found out. She would leave him, he knew, whatever he had thought before. She wouldn't go on peeling her potatoes in his kitchen. And she would take his children, one by one, out the door.

Deena came into the living room, picking up a child's shoe, a doll, and a fuzzy animal from the floor. She came and sat on the ottoman near him. She added a partially unraveled ball of yarn that lay at her feet to the collection of other childhood items already in her lap. Spare and crisp, she was, all finished with babies. How well she dressed now, he thought, in the clothes of a woman who had no tiny hands clutching at her.

"How was your day?" she asked him.

"Good," he said. Her hand rested on the arm of the chair. He covered it with his own.

"I've got a Monopoly game pending," he said, pointing toward the stairs.

"Doesn't that go on for hours and hours?"

"I've got a new short version," he said. "I deal out the cards so that we both start with lots of monopolies. We can kill each other off in half an hour that way. Also, I encourage reckless play." He laughed.

She leaned back on him in his chair. One hand was on his thigh. "She's a good kid," Deena said.

It wasn't adultery, Deena, I know it might seem like it, but it wasn't what people think of when they think of adultery.

"Go play," she said. "We'll eat in about forty minutes."

Her hand moved gently along his thigh. "Love," he said, in a voice with ragged edges. She raised her fingers to his mouth and he clutched for them desperately.

Fifteen

SHE began to strip the bed for the second time that day. She lifted one corner and pulled it away slowly, watching the pink and cranberry flowers disappear from the surface of the mattress. Halfway through, she paused. How would Paul react when, tossing laundry into the machine on Saturday, he found two sets of sheets? Wasn't he more likely to notice that, than that they had been used illicitly? Did the sheets hold any real evidence of their deed? She held the soft pile of percale to her face. The sharp smell of newly-washed filled her nostrils. After all, they had been on the bed only a few hours, and Paul had never been an observer of detail. She stretched the sheets back across the mattress, refitted the corners, and finished making the bed.

So David had a gun, after all, she thought as she adjusted the TV color knob for higher contrast. Poor Mona, talking on the telephone, thinking she was all alone, but David was in the next room, hearing every word, ready to pounce on her. He had reached over, pulled open the drawer of the occasional table: a tight close-up of a hard, black gun, with David's hand stroking the barrel as it still lay in the drawer. What had he overheard? Amy had not had the sound on for days. She had thought Mona would leave David. Mona opened her closet and scanned its contents. The camera moved in on a suitcase on the top shelf. Mona's hand tightened round the handle, her face shone, beatific. The credits rolled by silently. Amy turned it off.

So she had been right. Mona was thinking of leaving. But it would take weeks. It would drag on forever. There would be scenes in the sleazy motel where Mona thought to escape, then scenes in the hospital after David had come looking for her, bullying her, beating her, and maybe blowing her brains out.

Her own luggage was under the bed. She lifted the bedspread and groped till she found the two brown cases. Paul's initials, not hers, were stamped in simple, clear gold and were much larger and more visible than she had remembered. It would not be fair, she thought, to take his suitcases, possessions that predated their marriage. She had a few canvas bags, somewhere, but they were handbags, hardly large enough to hold more than one change of clothes, at best.

But she was not leaving today, anyway. Today was a normal day. Paul would return at the normal time. They would do the usual things.

Unless he did notice. Unless he grew outraged and exploded. Would he throw her out? She pulled back the bedspread again, puffed the pillows, smoothed the bottom sheet and then the top sheet. At night we're so cold, she thought, he never looks. We flip out the light, jump into bed, and pull the covers round our necks. She checked again, and then again. The sheets smelled clean.

So, it would be fine.

Although there was the V-8 in the refrigerator. He'd never questioned that. Who did he think sprinkled rock salt on the front path? Had he assumed an invisible, benevolent landlord? Had he simply failed to notice? How was she to know that he wasn't compiling evidence, like the detective who knows who his criminal is, but who is unwilling to make the arrest until he has a watertight case for the jury? And when would he spring it on her? Tonight? It was possible tonight would be the night. And Mrs. Martin. Why had she so conveniently forgotten Mrs. Martin? All the old woman had to do was to pick up the phone and dial university information. She would be connected to Paul's desk within seconds. There's a truck, she would say, trying to disguise her baby thin voice. A mail truck. It stops almost every day. For an hour. Thought you might like to know. They should not have used the bed. Then the question of the sheets would have been nonexistent. She stopped pacing and stood in front of the mirror. Well, of course, she looked no different. She was no fool. She knew that. Her voice, though, completely involuntarily, might begin to give her away. The lighting in the bedroom was terrible, and the air much too close, she thought. She moved through the kitchen, past Marissa in her crib, and out into the living room. One solution would be to let Paul talk. He was always saying that she never said anything anymore. If she just shut up, she wouldn't say anything stupid, and he wouldn't think she was behaving any differently. She wouldn't look at him either, because eyes were said to give people away.

How would she explain if Mrs. Martin called him? Where would she begin? Yes, the mailman stops in. I didn't mention it because I didn't think it was important. It's important to Mrs. Martin, because she has nothing else to do all day, that's all. I felt sorry for him, it's so cold, and he's always asking after the baby.

Or she could just tell him, couldn't she? I'm sleeping with the mailman. It had such a crude sound to it. But Paul hated euphemisms, so there was no point in beginning obliquely, with phrases like, "I haven't been happy being alone all day." Better to tell him outright and get it over with. He would think, Amy is a crazy lady. She invites men in off the street.

And what would he do? So eminently rational, he was. Liked

to work things out in advance. Check the proper sources, make the appropriate calls. Inevitably there would be the two fingers pressed to his forehead, a hand passed distractedly over his beard, and it would be done. "And Rissy," he would ask. "What were your plans for her?" He would care about that. Enough to fight her? To follow after her? Would she forever be listening for footsteps, wondering, as Mona did, when the masculine hand and weapon would fall on her?

She had slept with him once: was it an affair yet? Suppose Marissa never slept through a lunch hour again. It would be over, finished, and it had hardly been an affair at all. It was only this one time. She rushed back to the bedroom and pulled the larger suitcase halfway out from under the bed, then quickly forced it underneath again. She knelt, her head and arms on the bedspread. Should she pose like this at his feet and beg forgiveness? She looked at her watch. He would be home in only a little more than an hour. She would not be ready to face him.

She hadn't realized that an affair in his bed would seem so final. So separate from all that had come before. Yesterday it was not an affair, today it was. For Joe, it would be different. It had not been his bed, his home. He might shake it off.

She would go out.

Back in the bedroom, she tossed garments from the closet shelf. She would layer herself up. Protect herself from the cold. You started with a thin sweater, she knew, a flat knit, then a turtle neck, then a heavier sweater. Would she need even one more? she wondered, eyeing the pile she was amassing on the floor. Her fat sweater, too. She'd layer that over the whole mess. And what good was an East Coast jacket, cut slim and trim ("This one shows off your figure beautifully," the saleswoman had told her), if she couldn't put all this under it? She climbed down and gathered the sweaters into her arms. How would she manage this?

She felt the wind sneaking round the edges of the back door and heard the rattle of the kitchen window that accompanied every gust. Even the interior of the house felt treacherously cool now, after having had the window open. She would jack the thermostat up and wait till things warmed again. Give the temperature a chance to level out. Anyway, how would she dress the baby to tolerate this weather?

She knelt beside the baby's crib. The blanket moved almost imperceptibly up and down across the infant's back. How she would have liked to have lain down with her, to have put her own face onto that sleeping baby's back, or face, or belly, to move with the gentle breathing, to be sure it went on ceaselessly. She wanted the noise of baby breathing to pound in her ears. She would project it by remote microphone, if she could, into the far corners of the room, as the obstetrician had with the fetal heart sounds in his office. She would have crawled into the crib if she could have been certain it would not collapse with their combined weight. She needed to know that the rhythm of inhalation and exhalation would go on forever. Her hands pained her, clenched fiercely as they were about the bars.

Marissa lay curled, still, at three months, like a little baby monkey, soft as a teddy bear. Amy's own mother had called her Teddy Bear. "Teddy Bear," she whispered through the bars, "I can't take you out. I'm sorry. We'll try some other day."

"Will I always be your Teddy Bear?" had been the beginning of the ancient litany she exchanged with her mother, and always, there was the reply, "Forever and ever and ever." "Past forever?" Amy would ask. And "Past every forever and beyond" was her mother's unfailing response.

The baby opened her eyes, stretched, wrinkled her face for a complaint call, but saw Amy facing her through the bars. "Hi," Amy said, and the baby face relaxed and smiled. "Hi, Teddy Bear," she said and put her hand through to pet her. No crying. How much better it was to be there for the awakening, than to be

summoned imperiously from another room. She had missed so
many awakenings by hiding from this still primitive creature while
she slept. She ought not to have been so fearful. There was this
pleasure in it, too. She might bring a book sometimes and read on
the floor next to Marissa's crib, so as to be right there, to watch
her open her eyes and become a creature of this life.

She met Paul at the door. "Doesn't she look lovely?" she asked
him, holding out a baby attired in velour.

"She's wonderful. Is little baby going jogging in her warm-up
suit?" he asked in mock baby tones.

"We've played dress-up all afternoon," she told him. She
showed him the piles of clothes, organized, as she explained, into
Too Small, Just Right, and Too Big. "She hasn't even worn very
many of these," Amy said, indicating the Too Small pile. "She's
so much bigger than she was, but you don't see the changes, living
with her daily. I didn't know she'd have outgrown all these."

"Rissy," he said, lifting her over his head, then bringing her
down to touch noses, "you're growing too fast."

"Not too fast," she corrected him. "I need to have her larger."
She was growing and would keep growing no matter what anyone
said. She thought it was important to remember that.

Sixteen

AMY circled the date in the small calendar of her check record, just the way they did to your courtesy card in the supermarket when you cashed a check. February 26th. Today's visit. February was quite filled with him. January was sparser. And March? He might disappear anytime. She might have seen the last of him.

She dialed Julia's telephone number. "The pajamas are marvelous," she told her. "What do I owe you?"

"Fifteen dollars."

"Do you think you could send another pair?" After those arrived, she knew she would ask for slipper socks, then booties for the baby, then leg warmers for herself. She was certain she could make enough requests to produce a steady stream of parcels. "It's so very good of you to help me out, this way," she told her sister. "With this weather, with the baby, it's almost impossible for me to go anywhere."

"I remember those days," Julia said. "Even in good weather, it's hard."

"Oh, it is," Amy nearly shouted into the phone, and she felt so joyful, suddenly, realizing that Julia actually understood and might

even understand about Eddie, that she considered telling her everything, but thought better of it and choked her laughter down, afraid
it might give her away. The effort started tears rolling down her
cheeks.

"I've always thought that the best stage in child rearing is pregnancy," Julia said. "Then, at least, you're the boss. If you want to
go somewhere, the child can't have a tantrum or try to talk you
out of it. After that, it's all kind of downhill. Eventually, they start
calling all the shots. You graduate from mother to slave fairly early
on, I'm afraid." She laughed. Amy contemplated whether she
would still be able to hear Julia if she were to unscrew the plastic
covering of the earpiece. "We're dying to see that baby," Julia
said.

A small sob crept out of Amy. "Maybe soon," she said. "I've
some things I need to work out first."

"What's the matter?"

"Nothing," she said, standing now, offering across the phone
wires the standard signal to indicate the end of their interview.

"Is it really nothing? Is it something about Paul? You sound sort
of ominous and scary."

"It's really nothing," she said, shifting from foot to foot to em-
phasize her impatience with the length of their talk.

She pressed her hand down on the receiver long after she had
hung up. Why did Julia laugh when she said those things about
child rearing? If it were true, it was a horrid picture to draw. And
if it weren't true, why tell her now while she was struggling so?

She dialed the Automobile Association and asked for the travel
department. First destination? the woman asked. Great Smoky National Park, Tennessee. And from there? Just up the Blue Ridge.
Side trips to the valley. Consider avoiding the Mississippi River
route because of potential spring flooding. Spring, she thought.
Was it possible there was this much snow here, but if she got in
her car and drove only two days she would be in spring? Winter

and spring on the very same planet. The very same hemisphere. Same country. She wasn't sure how many states lay between Minnesota and Tennessee, but she could envision perfectly Minnesota's position in relation to the rest of the continental United States. She would be able to draw a rough outline of the country, then place a star where Minneapolis was. She would annotate such a sketch with red letters spelling out, "You are here" and a set of red arrows pointing south, away from the star. It was something she might consider putting in the notebook some time. She could take the notebook with her, of course, if she were ever to go East. That way, she could use it as a travel journal and record everything she did. The sketch would be like a title page to that part of the notebook. But she thought she might wait till she was on the road before she really began. In the Smokies, she could draw a new map. A new "You are here" label. There would be no need for the new pajamas on the trip, she didn't think. The first day's travel could get a person quite far, if you left early enough and really pushed, driving till it was time to sleep, traveling as deep into the spring as you could.

She pulled the pillows from under the bedspread and curled her back into them, notebook in hand. One person could quite luxuriate in the space available in a double bed. But it was odd, she thought, that it had become the custom for two people to share such a small-sized unit. Two single beds would be far larger. And then you would have room on both sides to fling your arms about, or your legs, even. You could go beyond your half. A little shelf, she thought, would be handy. A simple extension off the side — it could be folded into the bed somehow (like a trundle bed, slid underneath, perhaps?) during the day. Then, as the other person stretched and pushed over onto your side, you could just drop off into the little tray and sleep perfectly well.

She refilled her fountain pen with care. She didn't have to do that every time she wrote, for often she used very little ink, but she liked it to be topped off that way. She enjoyed watching it fill, liked the little sucking noise it made, and especially liked to wipe the point afterwards, stroking it with a small square of white cotton. Also, she was quite certain that if you filled it right before beginning to write, the ink flowed better as you began; you didn't have that momentary dry quality.

She lifted her finger up and down along the pen. Like a flute, the pen was an instrument of expression. It was true that some of the things she thought about writing in the notebook sounded slightly trite or silly, but they were haunting phrases, lost motifs from another era. The words had a way of coming into her head already phrased, like captions under a posed Victorian picture. The longer she kept the phrases in her head, playing them over and over, the more intense the accompanying pictures became. *A Marriage Gone Awry.* That was one of the more persistent ones. That one had come into her head picture and all. All the pictures were sepia, not at all like the TV faces. She admitted to a certain fascination with a color screen for the way it made public the pores of the actors, showed you where the grey sideburns ended and the black hair of an actor's head began, or emphasized the brassiness of a character through her foolish preference for bright gaudy silks. But the sepias she composed — or remembered (they were so vivid she must have remembered them) — had layers of emotion that made you crawl inward, inside a character, and never left you hovering about on the surface. The sepias looked passive and posed: their message was delivered in absolute quiet, by barely perceptible implication only. The marriage one consisted of a man and a woman. He sat at a desk, off to the right, pen in hand, his eyes on his paper. She was off to the left, turned slightly left, hands clasped in front of her but held down low. The longer Amy watched, the more she realized that the woman's expression was not the vacant stare it had first seemed. She could see that she was not only contemplative, but that she was also firm and determined.

She was, in fact, willful. He might go on at his desk as if nothing had happened, but she had decided something. This realization of the woman's firmness made Amy hesitate to include it in the notebook, for on trying to capture that strength, she stumbled over phrases like "The die is cast." She would have preferred something less overdone. Something about the paradox of soft cherubic cheeks and strong inner resolve. But phrases she recognized as hackneyed always crowded all else out. She would whisper the tired phrases to herself, and the old photograph would instantly reappear. The woman's hair was piled magnificently in the manner of the times. After viewing the picture, Amy sometimes examined her own hair, swooped it up to the top of her head. Quite unlike her marriage woman. She blamed that on the difference in the times: no central heating back then to dry hair out. Only in Minneapolis could one die, she thought, from tissue death caused by too much oil heat. She reached for hand lotion.

The New Family had been another phrase, complete with visuals, that had occurred to her. This was more typically Victorian, she thought. The woman, wearing (as in all the pictures) a dress with a high lace neck, sat in a spindly-legged armchair, baby in long flowing christening robe in her lap. Husband behind chair, his hands on the woman's shoulders. Their faces were empty in this one, not at all like the marriage one. And when she kept it long in her head, she saw that although the man's hands appeared to rest on the wife's shoulders, his fingertips were raised up and were not touching her at all.

The ones with the pictures she never put in the notebook. They were too histrionic. And there was Paul, too, to think of. He'd become pushy lately, wanting her to call people, wanting to control her more. He might choose now (how could she know?) to begin checking up on her through her writing. She no longer kept the notebook in their shared desk. That was one protection. She kept it in a purse she didn't use and kept the purse in her closet. Now

Paul might read something he found in her desk, if he just came across it, she supposed — although even that was unlikely — but she was certain he wouldn't search for something. Looking through purses and all, that just wasn't him. She might have gotten a locking notebook, like the diary she had kept the year she was thirteen. But that kind of thinking was foolish, she reminded herself. Paul would not read it. Wouldn't even open it. Lock or no lock. That was the way he was. He could come upon letters and notes, or whatever, and if they weren't his, he didn't even seem curious. She had none of that coolness. When letters arrived for Paul, she'd often hold them up to the light, not because she hoped to glimpse something of a secret life, but because the closed envelope seemed an affront, like a childhood dare. She found it odd that he showed no particular interest in ripping open his own mail. Often as not, he handed it over to her, as if he couldn't be bothered. After a while she began opening some of it before he got home. Long ago, she had worried that one day she would chance upon some secret. An evil thought. A secret longing. Then, when she had those expectations, her hands had sometimes shaken. The letter would go down on the kitchen table, then up again into her hands, then down again. Now she ripped letters open without worry. If the return address intrigued her, if she wanted to know what the correspondent had to say, she opened it. If there were secrets, he housed them elsewhere. The top of the fountain pen rested lightly on her lower lip. She looked at her own fingers spread in an arch, fanlike, away from the pen, poised as though over a transverse woodwind. Where was her flute? Somewhere. Had to be. She grasped the pen more firmly. Prepared and ready to write. She did think, even with Paul's restraint, that she ought to be restrained as well. She might just hang onto those marriage and family phrases for a while, before they went into the notebook. So she could be sure he wasn't looking for them.

And a funny thing: the ideas occurred to her at the strangest times. Very often when she was caring for Marissa. And then it was virtually impossible to do anything about them. Nursing, for instance. She couldn't just pop up and go to the closet and retrieve the notebook. So she weighed each one, repeated it, listened to it, watched if it had a picture attached to it. One time she had been changing Marissa, and one had come to her. She had held Marissa's ankles in her hand at the time (they were so small then, she could hold them both easily in one hand), lifting her bottom off the surface of the changing table as she wiped it with a nursery-print washcloth. *Someone Took Care of Us All* came into her head. And, almost instantly, there was the picture. A picture of a family, posed in front of a large home. Lined up on the front steps. In the back row was the mother, her arms extended round the shoulders of as many of her children as she could encompass (this photograph was more informal than the others, and in fact, she added a line below the title, *Family Summer House*). The first few times she saw the picture, the exact number of family members changed somewhat, but eventually she settled on seven sons and daughters, all with spouses, and most of the women pregnant. At their feet were rows of children arranged in size order, with the smallest sitting down front. The youngest infants were displayed in their mothers' arms. The patriarch, she assumed, had been the photographer.

Eddie delivered the package from the Automobile Association the following Monday.

"Going somewhere and not telling me?" he asked her as he handed it over.

"You know about it. It's for the Virginia trip."

"You're really going, then?" he said as they walked toward the kitchen together. "For how long?"

"That depends," she said and paused. "Are you coming?" she asked him quietly.

"Would that I could, Love." He jiggled a bell that hung above Marissa's head in the playpen. The baby stopped moving suddenly, her dark eyes darting in all directions. He rang it again, and Marissa focused directly on the bell. "Atta girl," he said. "You're so pretty today in your pink dress." He reached a hand toward the baby, and she grasped at his fingers. "My pretty girl's going to take a trip soon, isn't she?" he crooned down at her. "Going back home, she is."

"Would it be possible?" Amy asked from behind him.

He turned round to face her, but she had already turned away, busying herself with table settings. "Ame," he said and put both hands on her shoulders. Gently, he turned her toward him. "Ame," he repeated, "I would like to. But it's crazy." He lifted her chin with his hand. "Very crazy."

"I know," she said. "It was just a joke. A funny idea." She disengaged herself from his hands and sat at the table.

"You ought to go, though," he said, pulling out a chair. "You need a break. You could see your relatives. And you need a break from the snow, anyway, don't you?"

She shook the blue-cheese-dressing bottle vigorously. Nothing happened. They filled the bottles nearly to the top and left you not the least little bit of room for any mixing. I might do this all afternoon, she thought, shaking my arm up and down, pretending to be achieving some end, and really only growing wearier and wearier. "You did want dressing, didn't you?" she asked. He nodded. "Blue cheese?" she further, needlessly, inquired.

"Yes."

She spanked the bottom of the bottle, but the congealed white and blue mass hung tenaciously to the inner glass walls. She slapped again, and with a funny little "fwop," the fat, uneven blobs began to slop all over the greens. A major lifework, she thought, getting it to spread evenly over everything without having the ingredients of the salad completely disintegrate under the pressure of twisting, turning, and scraping. She read the label now while he waited across the table from her. She wondered why she bothered to use the stuff at all. Marissa didn't have a ghost of a chance at survival in a world so dominated by chemicals. "Toxic levels of poisons have been found in the milk of nursing mothers." You could read about that kind of thing daily in the paper. We might as well all give up. The promise of Marissa's future: despair.

"We can talk about it," he said. "I'm willing to discuss it." Grown-ups did that, didn't they? They discussed things. They also told children that, when they were ready to do away with certain topics. Too bad Paul banned the discussion of soap operas over dinner. How much fun it would have been to regale him with the tales of Joe and Amanda. That would have been stimulating entertainment. You see, when it really came down to it, he just wouldn't leave his wife, Paul. They're all like that on the soapies, they talk big, expansive gestures, stolen kisses, special promises, but at the last, at the final moment, they won't leave. His wife's wealthy, or there are the children to consider, and it dead-ends, time after time. Paul would want to know the details: had he actually previously said he would go with her? Had she asked him point-blank before? Had they ever discussed his leaving his wife? She'd have to tell Paul, she didn't think they had. Perhaps she had missed that episode. And the promises she'd mentioned — he'd want to know about those. What were the promises? That everything would be all right, Paul. A bit vague, he'd say.

Eddie had her hand in his now. "Amy," he said. "The salad looks terrific. Do you want me to serve?" She pushed the salad toward him.

"Who do you think we are, Joe?"

"I don't know," he said as he filled her plate. "We'll have to talk, I guess."

"Maybe tomorrow?" she asked.

"Maybe tomorrow."

"You'll come tomorrow?"

"Yes," he said, "although that isn't a guarantee I can talk about anything."

They held hands across the table before they ate their chef's salads.

They had turned the corner into March. Paul pulled the New Hampshire birch trees, bent nearly double under their white, white snow, from the Sierra Club calendar. Moss on the side of a tree and tiny blue scilla poking through forest grass became the new image. He rehung the calendar on the wall next to the kitchen table. "Another month of winter down," he said. It was a particularly dreary day, and although there was only a light snowfall, the sky seemed closed over and forbidding. At nine o'clock there was no more light in the sky than there usually was by very late afternoon. Amy examined the ice on the windows. She ran her fingernail along the glass, cutting through the ice trees so that their tops were severed from their lower sections. Like trimming the Christmas tree so it will fit in the parlor, she thought. Paul had trimmed their tree that way. ("The ceilings seemed so high, I was sure it would fit," he had said.) She pressed a fingertip to the ends of the feathery branches, leaving circular images behind: ornaments. Small round crystal decorations for her trees. She opened her mouth wide and blew against the glass. Her breath clouded over her picture, then became clear again, fused in ice to the layers beneath it. If she were to really decorate the trees, with colors perhaps, with strands of sparkling colors, would it be better? And how would she decorate them? Markers would slip and slide and run in the ice rivulets. Tiny felt circles cut with a paper punch and strung together like cranberry and popcorn chains. But how to attach them? Surely not glue or Scotch tape. Thumbtacked to the window frames and strung from side to side across the glass? Minnesota had given a new motif to their lives. Paul had brought a real tree home this year. "Why did you buy a tree?" she asked him. "We've never had one before," she said as he struggled with it at the door.

"We've never had a baby before, either, but we have one this year, right? And it's not as though we're religious, you know."

"But a Christmas tree . . ." she began.

"Everyone here has a tree. And it's because of Marissa, too. This kind of thing is for children."

"She can't see it, Paul," she'd reminded him. "She's ten days old." Then he'd arranged the presents under the tree. Like a department store Christmas display where you know the carefully wrapped packages are really just empty boxes.

Blue scilla. She wondered if snowdrops and scilla could grow at all in Minnesota. "I thought you liked winter," she said to Paul.

"I do, but at some point it would be nice to have some of the other seasons, too."

"Three more months of this," she said.

"No," he said. "The days are getting longer." He pointed toward the calendar. "Are those the flowers we saw that time we camped?"

Seventeen

$\mathcal{A}$MY had the maps spread out on the kitchen table when he arrived the next day. They stood side by side and stared at them wordlessly. The Shenandoah National Park was brightly delineated in green. She had a foldout pamphlet for the Blue Ridge Parkway that had pictures and descriptions of all the interesting places to stop along the route. Under the photograph of the summit of Peaks of Otter, he saw the words, "Spring is slow to arrive along Blue Ridge Parkway. The forests are bare when dogwood blooms late in April."

"It might be early," he said, "even for Virginia."

"In the valley," she said, "it'll be spring. I know it will."

Perhaps, he thought. The maps covered the entire surface of the table. He folded a map, bending and unbending it, trying to find the proper sequence of moves that would bring it to its original configuration. She put her hands down on two maps. Guarding them, he thought. He picked up another and folded it, and then she too, reluctantly, began to fold one away. "It's a nice route, Joe. You didn't really look, did you?"

"No," he said. "What about Paul?"

"What do you mean?"

"Won't he go with you?" He watched her walk toward the refrigerator, then open it and stare inside. He thought about her electric meter clicking off dimes and quarters while she cooled the kitchen down that way. Then again, maybe the landlord paid the utilities.

"Lunch?" he asked her, and she looked toward him, as though she was surprised to see someone in her kitchen. And what am I doing here? he wondered. How did the postman get in? He watched the baby circling her arms as she lay in her infant seat.

"I made sandwiches," she said, turning back to the refrigerator and removing packages wrapped in aluminum foil. She handed them to him, and he placed them on the table.

"Sit down," he said, and she sat at the table across from him. "What's Paul like?"

"Don't, Eddie," she said.

"I'm sorry," he said, "but who we are has to do with them, you know. He's not a mean person, is he?"

"No," she said, "I guess he's a nice person."

"Deena, too."

"Do you love her?"

"Yes."

"I don't know if I love Paul."

"You and I," he said, "we ought to go back to our lives. Pick them up again. You and I can't be anything together."

"Lovers?" she whispered.

"Between twelve and one, weekdays? That's not being lovers. That's slipping out of the uniform and back in again. No time for lunch, even. Listening to the guys laugh about how Eddie's just one of the guys who gets laid at lunch."

"We can be friends, like this, like we are."

He shook his head. "Ame, we're wanting to be lovers, not

friends." In his mind, he saw them fly toward one another, embrace, and float weightlessly upward, naked as marble angels, then disappear.

"Do you think about what could happen to us?" she asked him.

"Yes."

"What do you think?"

"Everything. One day I think we'll go to Virginia forever, the next day I think we'll never see each other again. One time I lay awake thinking about us all having dinner together, the four of us, here, at your house, and we get to talking about Virginia, and Paul says he can't take the time off to go with you, and Deena suggests I drive you, and Paul offers the car, and everyone's real friendly. I say no, but they insist." He paused. "Then you get up to clear the table, and I follow you into the kitchen. We don't touch each other, but the air is charged like you wouldn't believe. We keep moving round one another, listening at the same time to them talking about the weather. Then we sit down for dessert, and I think about you and Deena sitting on either side of me, Paul not knowing, and . . ." Now it was he who looked away. "This whole thing is crazy, Ame."

"And when we're all sitting there," she said breathlessly, leaning toward him, "Paul doesn't notice a thing, does he?"

"No. And neither does Deena. You do, I do. I think about excuses to get you out of the room, but I never say them."

"Do you think about the trip, then, after they give their permission?"

"Yeah, I think, there's no rush now, we're going East together, and then I think about the trip. Without Paul and Deena, it's easier."

"What happens then?"

"We get in the car, Marissa in the front seat with us, and we start singing, like we're on a bus, going to summer camp. Jesus, Ame, it's nutty."

"Joe," she said, "I like the singing part, I do." She held her hand out to him, and he kissed each finger. "What else?" she prodded.

"You nurse the baby. Next to me, there on the front seat." Her fingers moved over the back of his hand, brushing the dark hair back and forth.

"I probably wouldn't, you know. It's not safe. I'd make you stop somewhere."

"If she started to cry, I'd look for a spot to pull over, and I could sit and watch you nurse. That would be even better." He watched her breasts rise and fall with her dark-sounding sigh.

"First day," she said, "I thought we'd go as far as we could, so we'd get to warm weather faster."

"That's fine," he said.

"I'm not bringing warm pajamas, even."

He pulled the curtain back from the window next to the table and ran his hand along the ice, outlining the curves with his fingertips. He watched her fingers drumming lightly on the formica surface. "I'll keep you warm," he said, and he moved his hand to cover and still hers.

"Your fingers are cold," she said.

"Warm them," he said, and she wrapped his one chilled hand with her own, then held it to her chest. Together they watched Marissa, not each other.

"Will we camp?" she asked him.

"If it's good weather, we should. We can save money that way, but with the baby, we won't want to if it rains. Then once we're out there, I'll get on the postal list, and it won't happen right away, but eventually, I'll get in."

"I could teach," she said. He nodded.

"We'll never get a house, though. Nobody can anymore." He turned toward the ice, then eased his hand away from hers. "It's pretend, Ame. I can't call Deena from a phone booth in Kentucky and tell her to break it to the kids."

"I know."

Marissa had begun to cry, a relentless, piercing cry. "She's been fed," Amy said, "just before you got here."

"I'll hold her," he said. But she would not be calmed. He rocked her, paced with her, but she continued to scream.

"Do you think she's sick?" Amy asked

Eddie stopped pacing. "I think she needs putting to bed, Amy." He had to raise his voice to be heard above Marissa.

The baby had not done this in a long, long time, Amy thought. Her own fingers felt stiff and inflexible, much too rigid for holding a baby properly. "Shall I try to nurse her, again?"

"I say try anything, but I'm sure she wants to sleep," he said, and handed the baby over to her mother. Marissa would not nurse and only thrashed about at the nipple.

"Let's try napping her," he said. He carried the infant to her crib. Marissa squirmed and wailed a few seconds, then closed her eyes and slept. Eddie took Amy's hand and kissed it. "Just you and me," he said.

Amy thought: how nice it would be to put my feet up and relax for a few minutes.

Eighteen

*W*AS twice an affair?

There was no time for lunch, and so again she handed him his sandwich at the door. From the top step, she watched as he walked down the path. A woman with a backpack skied hand in hand with a child along uncleared sidewalks and lawns. Eddie waved to them. For a moment, Amy thought the pack, poised high on the woman's back, was a baby. He turned toward Amy as he entered the truck but did not wave, did not signal. She stayed on the step, coatless, till she could see the truck no more.

The window in the bedroom still stood open. If it weren't for Marissa, she might open more windows, just once, and only briefly, so the awful smells of winter might be carried away. She opened the back door and leaned out into the cold air. There were bird prints which led right to the door, then back down the stairs again. How strange that a bird would venture so close to human habitat, she thought. Why didn't all the birds leave Minnesota in winter? How many foolish ones had been left behind to try to survive? She would put out crumbs and maybe even some fat for them. In New Haven, their neighborhood had been home to so many bird feeders that Amy had thought migrant birds were seduced by Best Wild Bird Seed Selection into thinking staying north was preferable to flying south. In early morning and in late afternoon, there would be a marvelous cacophony of bird words rising from all the yards. Saturday afternoons in winter, she and Paul would sit by the window, steaming French onion soup before them, fascinated by perch fights and other bird rituals. In this house she would not even be able to see a feeder for all the coating of ice on the windows. Eddie had suggested she scrape the windows with a putty knife, but the ice would only grow back. It might be easier just to wait till spring. By then, the birds would no longer need to be fed.

Another winter, when Marissa was older, she might show her the bird tracks. Summon her to the door, and begin to teach her to distinguish bird tracks from other animal tracks, and finally to distinguish cat and dog and skunk and racoon tracks from one another. They would pull on boots and follow the tracks till they disappeared into the bushes.

Now, however, Marissa was not a transportable item. She did not walk. And although Amy knew that some people probably skied about with babies in back packs, she thought it a dangerous escapade. Driving, too, was dangerous. If it were just herself, it would be different. She could get in the car and go somewhere, but with a baby, it would be irresponsible. She had never driven in Minnesota snow. She had dealt with snow and ice in New Haven, but it wasn't like this. There were places here where the roads were so narrowed, you felt as though you were in a tunnel because of all the snow piled high on the sides. Paul said that ice was ice no matter where you were, and you still just rocked the car back and forth and eased the accelerator out slowly. There had been some bad winters in New Haven, too. Not like this, of course, but there had been ice storms, and she had navigated through them. She might try a short trip, just to see if she could handle it, then just turn round and come back.

There was, though, the possibility of getting stuck somewhere. And once you were really stuck, you needed sand and maybe even a small rug to throw under the wheels for traction on the ice. She had read in the paper about people getting stranded on highways. (She knew that was in blizzard conditions, but still, you had to extrapolate, and out here blizzards sometimes blew up out of nowhere. Out of simple predictions of light snowfall.) She could not, in good conscience, take a chance at going out without sand with a baby in the car. How long would it take for an eleven-pound baby to die of the cold? A journey out was an idea best forgotten.

Then this occurred to her: what did Paul do about sand? Wouldn't he have some in the trunk? Didn't he protect himself against emergency? Even in New Haven he had had all that equipment in the trunk: telescoping snow shovels, sand and scoops and door mats and salt. She was sure there would be sand in the trunk. She would get ready to go out but check the trunk before she actually started the car. A short trip. Very short. And she'd stay in residential neighborhoods, just in case she did get stuck, as an extra precaution. She'd ring somebody's doorbell if she had to.

She prepared herself and the baby for the journey outward as easily and carefully as if she had done it twice daily her whole life. She changed the baby into a one-piece sweater suit, pulled on her own flannel-lined jeans, a tee shirt for a layer of warmth, a cotton shirt, and a red crew neck sweater. With the baby still churgling and gasping at the first breast, Amy dialed Ellen's number.

"Would you like some company for a while?" Amy asked her. She would have a real place to go. A destination. I spent the afternoon at Ellen's, she would be able to tell Paul. We drank tea, we talked. She would tell him what they talked about. They might laugh together about Ellen's feather-headed ideas.

She pulled on the brown leather boots she had bought for the cold Midwest just before they left New Haven. They still had their delicious brand-new leather smell. She had some trouble locating her keys, for it had been so long since she had used them, but they hung on a hook near the back door, highlighting the route to the car. As she eased herself out the door, gliding carefully along the icy wooden steps, clutching at the railing for stability, a gust of wind rose, gathering itself from far off down the end of the backyard. It struck at her, knocking the breath from her, starting her gasping. The baby, surprisingly, did not cry. Amy pressed the infant's face gently against her shoulder. The tops of the tall evergreens seemed to spin round and round in the wind like a child's top, then came to a sudden eerie standstill. Amy glowered into the stillness, hunched up her shoulders, and prepared for a new attack. She took the steps slowly, lowering one foot and then the other onto each new level, until she touched sidewalk. In the driveway, her stride was wide, so she might brace herself and her child against the wind. She counted each step as she moved along. Fifteen steps from staircase to garage. From the kitchen window it had seemed as though it would be many more than that. The garage door glided quickly along its tracks, rising lightly out of her hand. She settled Marissa into the bucket-shaped car seat. Two plastic diapers and one dry jump suit. Not likely to last Marissa very long. It was downright reckless, she thought, taking a baby out in weather like this, with so little to change her into, and only the hood of her snowsuit to protect her head from the cold. She turned the key in the ignition, and the motor roared in response. She laughed. "Reckless," she said aloud, and more laughter rolled through the car, filling up the dry, empty spaces. She released the emergency brake, and the car surged backward, gliding first over concrete, then ice, more concrete, more ice. She felt the alternations beneath her; changes coming up at her through wheels, through pedals. "Reckless," she repeated when she had reached the end of the driveway. She remembered then about the sand. She had not checked to see if there was sand. "We'll be all right," she told the already slumbering baby. "I've driven in ice and snow before." She turned on the radio, rolled down her window and laughed all the short distance to Ellen's.

A hard-packed patch of ice held fast to the left rear wheel of Amy's car. Amy rocked the car back and forth, and it slipped forward again, through the high banks of shoveled snow on either side of Ellen's driveway. She moved the gearshift slowly between reverse and first. And why not keep going? she thought. Her hands were steady. She was perfectly fine. Why not see where else she could go, what streets, what towns she could drive?

Ellen waved vigorously from the back door. Her hair grew lighter and lighter every time Amy saw her. Today, against the whiteness of winter outdoors, Ellen's head gleamed white blonde. A Scandinavian convert, Amy mused. I surrender, she thought, anchoring the car with the parking brake. I am discovered. Now she would have to stay, but not for very long. She would move on, go somewhere else, taking the inevitable one step at a time.

Ellen embraced her, virtually carrying both mother and baby into her home.

"You'll have to excuse what a mess the house is in," Ellen informed Amy while she took off her coat. "You'd think with all this time indoors that I'd get to it, but I never do." She took Amy's coat and tossed it over a chair. Ellen made no reference to Amy's courageous venture. There was no banquet table prepared for celebration, no brass quintet for welcome. Amy felt too jumpy to sit down. She had done it: she had taken her baby and put her in the car and driven here. A small flute flourish would have been simple and sufficient.

"I've got this new tea set," Ellen said, "that I've been just dying to put to use." She opened the china cabinet and lifted out her cups and saucers. Amy reminded herself that, in absolute terms, she had done nothing extraordinary. She had only done what everyone else did a dozen times a week. "We got these last week at the City Fest

Crafts Show," Ellen said as she arranged place settings for each of them at the table.

"It's lovely," Amy told her.

"I'm so glad you've come, and not just because I can use the tea set, either," Ellen said. "I should have called you about the crafts show. You could have come with us. I didn't even think of it."

"It's all right," Amy said. "I wouldn't have come."

Amy eased herself into one of the dining room chairs. She held tight to the chair with one hand so she would not be tempted to jump up and run round the room. She was here to have a calm, grown-up social hour with Ellen.

"You've started going places now, haven't you?" Ellen's question was tentative. She pulled at her straight blonde strands as she slowly pronounced the words.

"I guess I have," Amy said, and, despite her efforts to seem casual about it, she began to smile, and a tiny laugh threatened to creep from behind her lips and to leap right into the middle of the room. She picked up one of the handcrafted cups and held it. "These are lovely," she repeated, and the smile formed itself comfortably round the compliment for a teacup. She remembered the icy steps, then, the ones she would have to reclimb to get home, and she wondered if they wouldn't be more difficult going up than going down. She saw herself tottering on the staircase with Marissa, and she recaptured her smile with a just audible gasp. "I'm doing a little bit at a time," she told Ellen.

"That's good," Ellen said. "Let me go make the tea so we can have something real to have a tea party with," she said and disappeared into the kitchen.

"Good baby," Amy crooned to Marissa when Ellen was gone. "Good of you to come with me," she whispered. The baby raised one hand, fingers reaching deliberately for Amy's face. Amy took the fingertips in her lips and kissed the baby palm.

"Would you rather have wine?" Ellen asked from the kitchen.

"All this early darkness gets to me. I start to think about cream sherry about three o'clock."

"Tea's fine," Amy said.

"I don't dare have a drink by myself because of that saying about how if you like to drink alone it means you're an alcoholic." Ellen stood in the doorway now, the handcrafted teapot dangling from her hand. "What I'd like to know," Ellen continued, pointing the teapot spout at her chest for emphasis, "is if I just want to drink alone but don't actually do it, does that make me an alcoholic?" She disappeared into the kitchen once more. Amy wondered if she oughtn't to have agreed to join Ellen in her cream sherry. It would be a celebration of her own passage through ice and snow. And she could grant dispensation to Ellen so she might have her little indulgence.

"What do you think about all this alcoholism stuff?" Ellen asked when she brought the steaming pot back to the table.

"I think that alcoholism, by definition, requires alcohol."

"But see, I'm not interested in scientific analyses. I'm more concerned with the philosophical questions."

Why were the philosophical borders of sin so muddled? I've wandered back and forth over them, she could tell Ellen, but I can't tell you where they lie.

"Do you ever drink when you're alone?" Ellen asked her.

"No," Amy said. "But you're right about the dark. And the cold." And she thought, Ellen would understand about Joe, but she said, "You shouldn't worry about it. About the drinking." She held her hands round her cup and remembered a time she had watched him across the table when he had said he would care for her, and the heat of the cup in her hands had spread through every part of her, and she had felt it, it's all right now, he'll take care of me, and she said, "Why don't we have a drink?"

"Oh no, the tea is fine. I'm just fine." Ellen poured more tea for the two of them.

"I'm not pregnant, again," Ellen said, as though they'd been discussing conception for the last ten minutes. "I just got my period last night."

Amy contemplated an appropriate response: you've a lifetime ahead of you, what's your rush? Or something nonverbal: a pat on the shoulder, perhaps, or an offer to let her hold Marissa, like the booby prize offered the maiden aunt. Why did genuinely important issues move her to clichéd gestures and nothing more? She settled on, "I guess you've been to a doctor about it."

"Yes," she said. "There's not supposed to be anything wrong with either of us."

If the doctor had looked inside her and seen unpatchable holes, would he have told her, or would he have protected her from the truth? "Maybe you should see another doctor," Amy suggested.

"We've been to three now. They all agree." Three doctors, thought Amy, add up to a truth.

"We have a bank account we set up for the baby way back when we first started trying. Now Doug wants to spend it on a vacation. I think he's resigned to being childless. He wants me to throw out the temperature charts."

"Maybe that would be helpful. Maybe you worry too much about it."

"I couldn't throw out the charts. It would be like saying the baby wasn't important. Like throwing the baby out, almost."

"Not if it made it more likely for you to conceive, though, and you don't know that it won't."

"Listen, there's no point in us both getting depressed," Ellen said. "Maybe this will be my month."

"Right," Amy said.

"It's these lousy foreshortened afternoons that get me down," she said, rising to turn on the light above their heads. "We're rapidly being overtaken by the gloom of evening."

She had not considered that it might be dark before she had a chance to return home. "Do you want to leave the baby with me for a while?" Ellen asked her. "You can do some shopping if you want." Amy had been thinking she might just sit there til Doug returned, so he could drive her home with Ellen following in their car. "If she doesn't need to be fed or anything. I'd like to hold her for a while, anyway, if you don't mind." Ellen already had her hands out for the baby. And then it was easier to hand her over, and to pull on her own coat than to explain that her resolve, along with her intestines and a major portion of her larger muscles had melted into custard-like consistency. She stood, holding herself upright by placing her hands on the table. "I won't be gone long," she said to Ellen, and the first few steps were wobbly, but they straightened out by the time she reached the door. And it wasn't dark yet. She could drive to a market and back in the semi-light, and she would be fine.

The final darkness came on suddenly. As she walked from the market to her car, the streets shone with continuous ribbons of headlamps. At red lights, engines behind her roared with impatience. When she didn't move immediately on green, a jarring and clumsy horn chorus roused her to activity. She thought of throwing her hands up and pretending to be stalled, forcing them all to go around her. But when those had gone past, there would be others, followed by more, all struggling to get somewhere as quickly as possible. She increased her speed, striving toward having her car move more gracefully with the flock. Near Ellen's house, where traffic eased and no one pushed at her from behind, she imagined how it might be if, with Marissa in the back seat, she suddenly heard a car speeding across the intersection. The cold, bloodless metal would fold round her, extracting her own blood for itself. She would be immobilized, unable to reach for Marissa. It would take very little force to twist and crush that small body. How would she tell Paul? She had chosen to take the baby out. After dark. Wasn't inability to make responsible decisions only one step short of criminal neglect? She turned on the radio and said aloud, "Marissa is not in the car." At Ellen's house, she would move the car seat from the side to the center. It was convenient near the door, you didn't have to crawl halfway across the seat to get at the baby, but safety would have to come first. Again, she repeated, "Marissa is not in the car," and the image of the twisted baby body began to fade. Anyway, she told herself, even if a car were traveling at high speeds, Marissa might escape injury in the center of the back seat. She took in a deep breath, held it, and set the parking brake in front of Ellen's house. Just the short distance home now.

Marissa had fallen asleep on a blanket on Ellen's floor. It was her night sleep, Amy realized, a hard, heavy sleep from which she was unlikely to wake in being carried in and out of the car. She wished the baby would stir, so she might talk to her. So she might hear her random noises in the darkened air. The lights of the car hit the ice of the front windows as Amy pulled into her own driveway. She saw Paul silhouetted, the curtain pushed aside, his arms spread wide and pressed against the window. The lights wavered across the bumps of ice, then left only blackness once again.

Crouched in the back seat, unstrapping the baby, she saw Paul at the back door. A light snow fell. *Winter Watch,* the scene might be called. Although with the snow and the red flannel shirt, loose and comfortable the way he liked it, she could not help thinking of *Santa Claus at Home.* And what would he see, looking out through the frame of the door, the spotlight on the back steps lighting her way? And who was she, woman with baby, walking through the snow? *Journey's End? Winter Scene?* Something about winter, certainly, but exactly what, she wasn't sure. Paul, still in shirt sleeves, stood at the side of the car.

"Shall I take her?" he asked, and Amy handed him the baby. She lifted a package from the front seat, then followed him into the house.

"I was worried," he shouted back at her. Once inside, he lay the baby in her crib. Amy closed the back door, pulling the locks to, one after the other. He came back into the kitchen. "You're all right?"

"Yes," she said. She dropped the brown bag she carried onto the table.

"You're all right?" he repeated.

"Yes," she said, her eyes firmly on the stove clock. It was just past six o'clock. There was no brass band here, either. Her travels, clearly, were of interest only to her.

"Did you eat?" she asked him.

"I was waiting for you. Sit down," he said and pulled one of the chairs from the table for her. "I made some tuna salad," he said. "Tell me where you went."

He pulled a chair next to hers, took her hand, and raised it slowly to his lips. "I'm glad you got out." The bristly ends of his beard tickled across her palm. She drew her hand back reflexively, rubbing the prickly sensation away against her pant leg.

"It's not such a big deal," she said, although she could feel a pulse, still, deep in her abdomen, which had begun pounding when she had first turned on the headlights to drive through darkened and only vaguely familiar streets.

"Where did you go?"

"A couple of places. I brought the baby to Ellen's house, and then I went downtown. I went to a couple of stores. I got these things at Town Square Market." She ought to have had them wrapped, she thought, although surely the storekeeper would have laughed at the suggestion of gift-wrapped vegetables. But then there would have been a festive note, although Paul, like the shopkeeper, would think her silly and unbalanced. Besides, calling attention to what she had done was foolish. Paul would just make a speech about it, talk about how she hadn't been going out, maybe even say, I told you so, see, isn't Ellen nice, too, and haven't you wasted a hell of a lot of time being housebound like an invalid, when all you've really done is had a baby? She handed the brown paper bag to Paul. Inside were smaller brown bags. He lined up the contents on the table: artichokes, endive, avocados, watercress, and kiwi fruit. He brought the endive to his lips and closed his eyes. She laughed. He was not going to lecture.

"You're easy to please, tonight," she said. "A bunch of fresh fruits and vegetables, and you're in heaven." She hadn't been thinking of him in the market. She had wanted to make a purchase, any purchase, to justify her extended wanderings up and down the aisles.

"Amy," Paul said, and she heard her name, encased in gold glitter and curlicues the way he said it, and she said to herself, well, now here it comes after all, the grand summarizing statement, and she drew herself into a firm and tight shape, but just a bit sparky, too, like the icicles that hung from the back door. He spoke quietly but slowly, as though each word had urged him to allow it equal time and emphasis: "You took the baby, and you went out."

She turned away and whispered, "It was easier than I thought." She did not tell him that car lights reflected off snow lit the black sky with a terrific brightness, for he would already know that.

"Endive and tuna fish?" he asked her. They stood simultaneously. "These are nice treats," he said.

"I should have thought about getting a steak. That goes better than tuna with all this stuff, doesn't it?"

"Tomorrow I could pick one up." He turned to her. "Unless you're going out again?"

"I probably will," she said. He kissed her suddenly, before she could back away. She had forgotten how that beard and mustache seemed to take over, to be in charge of her mouth for each kiss. She thought of Eddie, smooth, not-Paul. "I'm sorry," she said. She thought of Joe flinging open windows, and she saw him standing, still in the door to his truck, but now, he waved, and the truck rolled down the street, driven by some unknown force.

"What are you sorry for?" he asked and kissed her again.

"Anything," she said. "Everything." Now, she thought, now I will go down on my knees to him, but still she stood.

"OK," he said. "I'll forgive it all at once." He was smiling. Did he think her maudlin and idiotic?

"Do you really forgive it all?" she asked.

"Yes," he said soberly.

"Thank you," she said and turned quickly from him. At the refrigerator she forgot what she had come for. "Paul," she said, turning back toward him, "I took the baby, and I went out."

"I know," he said, but he did not come closer. "I'm glad."

"I am, too," she said. He had still not mentioned Ellen. And he had forgiven her. There might be other things to say to each other. There might be more to us, she thought.

"How shall we do the avocado?" he asked.

"Peel and slice," she said, "with lemon."

"I can handle that," he said.

As she watched Paul trim his beard next morning, she remembered her dream. She had been attending a lecture and writing in an enormous notebook. She had filled page after page, turning them as quickly as she could, but never quickly enough to keep up with the lecturer's words. The subject was beards. There were slides: beards in different shapes and colors. Beards through the ages. Sexual and social significance of beards in different cultures. She remembered a slide of a beard that was identical to Paul's. She had tried very hard to get down all the instructor had said about that beard, but she could not keep up. She had felt flustered and almost frantic. She had raised her hand to ask if he would cover care and trimming, and he had turned a cold countenance toward her, saying he had covered that in the last lecture. He had made her stand and give her name aloud, and everyone had turned round in their seats and stared. Where had she been for the last lecture? he had asked. She had stammered, said she didn't know there was another lecture, and he had noted something on a paper in front of him. Who's your dorm mother? he asked. My mother's dead, she said, and he had written something else down, too. Marissa's cry had wakened her.

Paul made funny faces at the mirror, puffing his cheeks out while he cut the stiff red and yellow strands exactly even. His beard never grew long enough to curl or twine gently. He liked that sharpness. He cultivated it with an almost daily trim.

She rinsed a washcloth at the sink, while his beard hairs fell all around her, then carried Marissa to the bed with her and began her morning feeding. Better to dream of lectures on beards, she thought, than to lie awake worrying about what would happen next. Between feedings, she had slept very well.

"How's Ellen, by the way?" Paul asked when he came into the bedroom.

"Not pregnant."

"I'd be surprised if she were. It's part of her life, even her self-image, I think, being unpregnant."

"Don't be cruel, Paul. She's very sad, poor thing."

"I didn't mean to be cruel," he said. "I was trying to be funny. I'm sorry. But you know, I really do wonder if she'd be any happier if she were pregnant."

"I don't think she'd be any more unhappy than she is now, and besides, people change."

"I know you think so." He was half in the closet, half out, selecting a tie. "Perhaps the real problem is that no one can predict how she'll change. What she'll be like afterwards." He was talking about *her* now, she knew. She didn't want to be referred to in the abstract.

He sat next to her on the bed. "Would you want to come down and meet me for lunch? We wouldn't even have to go out if you didn't want to. You could pack a lunch, and we could have a kind of picnic in my office. That way we could avoid the baby-in-the-restaurant problem."

Not lunch time, Paul, she thought. Not yet. I still need time. "I don't think so, today," she said.

"You're going to go out again, aren't you?"

She could hear the tightening in his voice. Maybe he was right, maybe she would never get out again. She could try, but she could make no promises. He was right to be worried. And if she never went out again, would he continue to forgive her so graciously? "I'll go out," she said, "but later. It's just that lunch is a difficult time for me." She stared down at the baby's mouth locked on her nipple. "There's the bath, and her feeding. By next week or the week after, her schedule may change enough so I can come at lunch. Don't worry about me," she said.

"I'm not." He adjusted his tie in front of the mirror. "Actually," he confessed, "I am, but I'll try not to." He turned to face her. "I've got to go in early this morning. I have an almost predawn appointment. I'll eat breakfast there."

"What kind of breakfast can you eat there?"

"Maggie's bringing in some doughnuts. She does, when there's an early meeting."

"OK," she said and curled herself a little more tightly round Marissa, so he would not think she wanted a good-bye kiss. She hated breakfast alone.

When she had finished mixing together eggs and cheese and noodles, she wondered how she had come so far without thinking. She had the makings of a noodle pudding in front of her, ready for the oven. Not the sort of thing she could hand to Eddie at the door. This is an affair, she said to herself, not a ladies' luncheon.

She roamed the apartment then, back and forth, over and over. The dusty wood floor under the coffee table bothered her more and more each time she passed through the living room. She found a rag and got down on her hands and knees to clear it away. Glad for the refuge of the mechanical motions of housekeeping, she dusted the entire room. She returned to the kitchen and put the pudding in the oven. What else was she going to do with it? Let three dollars' worth of ingredients go to waste? She had whipped the egg whites. If she didn't bake the pudding now, it wouldn't rise in that lovely way it ought to.

The telephone rang as she closed the oven door. It was Julia.

She was pregnant again. She sounded pleased, and so Amy wished her well. "The reason I called," Julia continued, "is that I was up all night thinking about how different it's going to be this time. With Mama dead, I mean."

Amy made a small noise to indicate she had heard. You could forget, she thought, with Julia's voice, that Mama was dead, but Julia, like Paul, was no lover of euphemism.

"I wanted to call you because you did it — I mean, had a baby without Mama to help. When Jamie and Rebecca were born, I had Mama, and I think of those early days, with her showing me things and doing things for me, and I get sort of scared thinking about it without her. I know I sound silly, because, supposedly, I should know how to do all those things already, shouldn't I? It's not like I'm a new mother." Amy made another noise of acknowledgement. "You did it, though, didn't you, and that makes me feel better."

"Yes," Amy said. "I did it." Past tense. Is it over, then? Have I finished, passed through the trial? When can I say I have survived?

"You sound like Mama on the phone," Julia said.

"You do, too."

"I'm afraid having this baby will make me miss her more. So I'm conflicted about it, you know what I mean?"

"Mama was already dead when Marissa was born."

"You're so much like Mama, Ames, the way you said that, so matter of fact. Remember how she always cut through to the heart of things? Remember how she used to tell everybody off?"

Amy remembered. She would have said, "Why'd you wait so long to get pregnant? You've been married five years. Now I'll be dead before the baby is born." That's what she would have said.

"She was so good with the babies. So free. She played with them, right from the beginning. As soon as I brought them home."

Amy thought of Marissa when she was born, of the skinny monkey-limbed baby. Her mother would have played ah-ah-baby with her. She had forgotten that game. You could do that with new babies, and they would gurgle and laugh. She had seen her mother play that way with neighbor babies, with cousins' babies. With Julia's babies and Marcy's babies.

"One other thing I thought of last night, Ames, was about the hospital."

"I understand that if you get a private room, it's really worth the difference in price," Amy said, and her laughter went askew, slipping and sliding out of normal bounds.

"I mean, it's the same hospital as where Mama died. The last time I was there was when Mama died."

"Put it out of your mind," Amy said. "I didn't used to think you could deliberately suppress things, but it really works. I don't think about Mama at all, except when you call. Think about the baby, not Mama. Keep changing the subject in your head."

"Maybe," said Julia. Amy could hear another conversation faintly over the phone lines. Two female voices, animated, sharing news in a rapid back-and-forth exchange. Laughter served as punctuation.

"Do you hear them?" Amy asked. "Do you hear the other conversation?"

"No," Julia said. "It must be just at your end." The interlopers were laughing again, sharing some hilarious secret. Amy could not distinguish their words. "Anyway," Julia said, "you did all right, didn't you, it wasn't too hard for you, was it?"

"No," said Amy, and her voice, mingled with those of the

strangers who shared her line, echoed in the mouthpiece. "Listen," she said, "I've this great noodle pudding in the oven I have to tend to, so I should get off."

"I'm sorry, Ames, calling like this, all depressed, in the middle of the day. I should have asked if you were busy."

"It's OK," she said. OK as long as you let me get off now, please, she said to herself. "We'll talk soon," she told Julia.

Why was Julia so worried about a third baby? Hadn't she gone through all the changes already? Hadn't she and Larry adapted from husband-and-wife mode to mother-and-father mode, permanently, long ago? So what would be different? A little less sleep, a little more work, more walking, more running, that was all. But the fundamental change had already occurred.

How she wished Julia hadn't begun with that hospital business. She had got Marissa and her mother all wound up with one another, just trying to explain to Julia how to separate them. The woman from Vital Statistics, that first morning in the hospital after Marissa was born, had confused her, too. She had hair black as onyx, lipstick red as a child's valentine, and a belly big as a baby's roly-poly toy clown. She was familiar-looking and dear to talk to, and Amy thought, if I had had a nanny, she would have looked just like this woman. And then she had thought, maybe this was my nanny, and I have forgotten. She had come to record information for the birth certificate. Paul had not arrived yet. Father visiting hours had not begun. Amy couldn't remember the baby's name at first. The woman offered to return, but Amy had laughed, told her it would come to her in a minute, and they had both laughed together, and Amy remembered how the woman's huge breasts had risen up and down with her laughter, and how her blouse had spread between the buttons. That hadn't seemed to bother the woman. She didn't try to close her blouse or conceal her huge, corset-like bra with her hand. Amy had admired that lack of gesture. Everything is happening so fast, Amy told her, and then she'd remembered, and she'd told her, the baby's name is Marissa, although saying it sounded very strange. *The* baby she had said, not *my* baby, and they hadn't brought her in yet, into her room, and she had begun to wonder what she would do with her when they did. And then the woman had asked her for information — mother's name, father's name, addresses, maiden name — and she had remembered the death certificate for her mother, and this woman looked so much like the woman who had asked her for the information on her mother. That was why she had seemed so familiar. Amy had suddenly had trouble catching her breath, and her next breath came, not as air, but as a sob, so big, she choked on it and felt herself shaking with the threat of more sobs, more shaking. She had wanted to put her head on the big woman's chest, but the woman had stepped back away from the bed and, with a peculiar grasping motion, she was pulling her shirt closed across her chest. "I'll get a nurse," she said and flew from the room.

The nurse had fluffed the pillows and pulled the sheet up. As she flung the curtains wide from the window, she said, "Don't you think it's time you got that little baby in here?"

Amy's tears were quiet by then, not the uncontrolled business of a few moments earlier. "Could I wait for my husband?" she asked.

"They won't let him in for two hours, honey. You're not going to let that baby starve, meanwhile, are you?"

"No," Amy capitulated.

"Good girl," said the nurse.

And so they had begun their life together.

Nineteen

EDDIE loved the noodle pudding. "I've a terrible sweet tooth," he said. "It's like eating cheesecake for lunch, isn't it?" He eyed his lunch fondly. "Tell me it's not evil."

"It's definitely not evil," she said, laughing. "It's even good for you. There's lots of protein in the cheese."

"There's milk and eggs in cakes," he said, "but I wouldn't call cake an ideal main course."

"Of course not," she said, "But noodle pudding is different. Believe me, you should just enjoy it."

"You've convinced me," he said, holding his hands up in mock protest. "I'll just have to force myself to eat."

She passed him the salad. "It's a health salad," she said. "Does that make you feel any better?"

"You're wonderful," he said and touched her lightly on the cheek. "How have things been going with Paul?" he asked.

"All right," she said. "I try not to think about us," she said, pointing her finger back and forth between the two of them, "and it goes all right." He had turned back to his pudding. She had not meant to hurt him with forgetting him. She touched the straight ends of his black hair that had grown just a little too long near his ears. "I have to. To survive the evenings, I mean."

"Of course," he said. "I have to do the same."

Did he sit at the head of a large dining room table, she wondered, with five children lining the sides? Five little girls who looked like some unknown, unseen woman. She thought of them, all dark and slender, all alike except for size, like a collection of nesting dolls. Children, he would say to them, you each tell what you did today. And then they would beg him to tell about his day, and he would tell them about a strange package he had delivered, or about a funny thing somebody at work had said. It would be news she could not hear. There, in his house, passing mashed potatoes, he would not think about her. His wife (in a dress with angel-winged sleeves and self-tie belt from the pages of Sears Roebuck?) would smile back. Or was she angry? Was she always angry at him, and was that why he took refuge here? And did he, by six-thirty when they were seated round that table, have stubble all over his chin? At noon, his face was smooth as Marissa's. She would have liked a list of concrete details about his other life: the TV shows he watched, the times his kids went to bed, and which stories he read to them. "What did you have for dinner last night?" she asked him.

"For dinner?" he asked, laughing. "Spaghetti with meat sauce, salad, and garlic bread."

The sauce Joe taught me how to make. I make it for my husband, he makes it for his wife. We never eat it together. Spaghetti intersections. They might plan one day to both make it, then both eat the same dinner in their separate homes, with separate spouses.

"I went out yesterday afternoon," she said as she cut herself another serving.

"Hey, darlin', that's terrific," he said. He pushed his plate aside and reached both arms out toward her. "With the baby?" he asked as he stroked her arm.

"Yes," she said. "I started too late, though. I don't like driving in the dark very much, and I got nervous after a while. Next time I'll go earlier. I think it'll be easier."

"It'll get easier. You've done the hard part, the first time out with the baby. I think it's super," he said, "and it'll be good preparation for your trip East."

Your trip. If he had decided not to go, why did he mention it at all? She had not brought it up. She drew her arms gently from under his touch.

"I won't do it alone," she said, and she poked her noodles with her fork till she had spread them in a thin layer all about her plate. "I don't suppose you'd really go, would you?"

"I don't see how I can. It wouldn't be terribly discreet, taking my vacation with my mistress instead of my wife."

"Mistress?" Amy said and winced.

"You don't like that word?"

She shook her head and scrunched up her nose. "Do you?"

"I guess it's old-fashioned, isn't it?" She nodded emphatically. "It sounds elegant to me. More elegant than some modern terms."

"To me it sounds harsh. Like 'kept woman.' I'd rather be a 'lover.'"

"It doesn't matter to me what we call us. You want to be a lover? Poof," he said, waving a hand over her, "you're a lover." Who are we really, Joe? He was silent, concentrating on something beyond them. "The baby's up," he said, and then she, too, heard Marissa's cry. "Well, you're a sometimes-lover, anyway," he said, laughing, and ran a hand through her hair. "When Marissa gives permission. I'll get her," he said, and he started for the space designated as Marissa's, with Amy following him. He leaned into the crib and patted the infant. "Almost time to go," he said, looking at his watch. "Did I get here late, or did we just linger over lunch?"

"A little of both, I think," she told him. "But you didn't finish your lunch, did you?"

"I don't think I could handle any more," he said. "It was wonderful, but it's awfully rich. Anyway, my wife thinks I'm putting on weight."

They turned away from one another.

At the door she said to him, "You're not putting on weight."

"I am, compared to what I used to be. Before we met." He kissed her. "Maybe it's the lunches. Before," he said, gesturing vaguely round the room, "I'd grab a yogurt or something. I'd even skip lunch some days." She looked into the corners toward which he had gestured, but they were empty corners, mere junctions of chipped baseboards and floors.

"You see a lot of babies in backpacks now," he said as he pulled on his boots. "I saw one the other day, she was a little older than Marissa. She held her head up really well, and it was precious, Ame, she was bobbing up and down, trying to see everything that was going on. Just bouncing up and down in the pack. You ought to get one of those and start walking with her. She can see the sights that way. It'll give you more freedom, too, get you out to the store once in a while." Boots on. Jacket on. Watch cap. Parka hood.

When he was halfway down the path, she tried to shout his name, but no sound came out. "Joe," she finally whispered when the truck was out of sight. "No one's going East, Joe."

She remembered what he had said as he buttoned his shirt: would that it could go on forever. She kept a picture of that one, his hands curved high over the button, just as he drew it through the buttonhole. *The Sorrowful Parting,* she called it. And there on the steps, another phrase came to her: *The Winter Affair.* It would be the subtitle for the *Parting* scene.

She had no backpack, but deep in the cardboard box that contained all the baby gifts, she found the front pack her sister Marcy had sent her. It was an elaborate contraption with snaps, straps, armholes, leg holes, and head supports. She had to practice swinging it round her shoulders with the infant right inside. Once Marissa was settled on her chest, Amy's hands were free. She could walk to the grocery store, she thought, and if she carried a shopping bag with her, bring home a small order, dangling it from her hand. At first the baby's weight, stuck suddenly to her chest, threw her off balance, and she walked mincingly over the ice patches, like a little girl in her first pair of patent-leather Mary Janes. Her nose and fingertips were brittle with cold. On the return, though, she arched her back more and found a comfortable walking stride. The wind was behind her, and she was less chilled. She forced as much air as she could from her lungs, then refilled them over and over with new air. She felt the cold, right down into her lungs, but still she wanted more of it. If only Marissa could do the same kind of air exchange, Amy thought, she could fortify herself with fresh breathing power. She hugged her front papoose to her chest, patting the padded bottom as she walked along. The air smelled only of the light white snow that had fallen early that morning. Marissa's cheeks were red when Amy brought her into the house. How beautiful she looked like that, touched by the cold. Amy kissed her baby's cheeks.

He dropped off a box of petits fours but did not stay. Did not even come in the door. He had an appointment, he said, but he didn't want her to worry about him. She told him about the front pack.

She lined up the cakes, each with a completely different frosted decoration, on her mother's blue cookie plate, made herself some tea, and put her feet up. She bit the first one in half and admired the tiny layers of cake and strawberry filling. There were only half a dozen, and she knew they wouldn't last long that way, so she got a thin-bladed knife from a drawer and began to slice the next one down. What wonderful servings they would have been for a doll's tea party, she thought. She must find a miniature tea set, so she and Marissa could have a tea party together one day.

She ran a fingernail through the ice on the window, then picked up the knife and scraped gently with it along the ice. The white trees slid away surprisingly easily under the metal. You want clear windows, Joe? she said to herself. I can give you clear windows. With the thin point of the knife she wrote her name, then Joe's, then scraped the whole window clear of ice. She sopped up the puddle that had formed on the sill with a kitchen towel and wiped the window as dry as she could, to forestall more ice formation. She was able to scrape three more windows before Marissa woke.

When she had bathed and fed the baby, she put her in the play-pen and waited, watching her till she became involved in batting the red and blue beads which hung suspended over her head. She pulled a chair to her bedroom closet and searched along the top shelf. A very different shelf than Mona's: no suitcases here. Under the piles of sweaters and sweat shirts she found the trim black case that housed her flute. She tossed the mass of earth-toned wools back on the shelf, then opened the box and held the individual silver pieces in her hands. She raised and lowered the keys. The muted clicks teased her brain: she listened for a moment, to catch the sounds of an orchestra tuning up around her, then chased the image away with a shake of her head. She assembled the flute with precision, twisting the mouthpiece to a spot in her memory. And yet she still only held it in her hands. When she felt the sounds of it so intensely in her lips, her tongue, and her teeth, that she could no longer resist but had to hear them aloud, she carried the wood-wind to the kitchen, wiped the denuded window once more, and lifted the instrument to her lips. She lasted through two octaves and began again. The second time was no less difficult, but also, she noted joyously, no more difficult. Marissa's eyes were focused unrelentingly on her while she played a fragment of a Bach sonata. She heard a phrase made by her own lips and her own fingers. It was a hint of music from within a jumble of notes. She tried again, and there it was, that singing musical phrase, followed, this time, by another, even warmer, phrase. She held the cold silver to her cheek, then cradled and rocked it in her arms. Flushed and puffing, she then made it through the entire exposition of the Bach. She replayed the two octaves with more ease and went on to three. Carefully, then, she took the instrument apart and dried it.

She picked Marissa up and held her, twirling round the kitchen to the sounds of Bach: dancers, together.

"Super," he said when she displayed her wealth to him, taking him on a window tour of the apartment and showing him the flute. He liked the blue velvet. Said he'd never seen a flute close up before. Then he put his arms round her and hugged her tight.

"See how well I'm doing?" she said into his chest.

"It's terrific," he said.

"And I'm not so crazy anymore," she said.

"You're not crazy," he said, holding her at arm's length, looking her over, smiling. "You never were crazy, either. Just never had a baby before, is all, darlin'." He drew her toward one of the cleared windows. "You might have snowdrops, you know. The last tenants, or even the tenants ten years ago, may have put them in. You have to keep an eye out." He turned back to her. "And you'll do fine," he said.

You're not subtle, Joe, she thought. Delivering your final instructions like that. "I'm not all better yet," she said and whispered, "A little longer, Joe." He kissed her.

So she wouldn't do any more, she thought. It was really simple. If he liked it better before when she couldn't do anything, she could be that way again. She could stay in bed. She could stop making lunches, too. That would make him aware things weren't right, wouldn't it? That's when things were most intense, she remembered. When she couldn't do anything.

When he was gone, she turned on the television and saw Mona lying nearly lifeless in a hospital bed. Amy didn't need the sound to know that David had shot her but had botched the job, leaving

Mona to vegetate for at least six weeks. "Don't take it so hard," Amy told the group of bedside hand-wringers. "They always recover." A moment later, she turned the knob, causing the images to fade into blackness. "Fools," she said to the screen and left the room.

That afternoon she took out the flute. She wanted to play it. She couldn't really help it. Probably there was some other way to keep him, she thought.

He heard a laughter in their meetings that was new. She wasn't so worried, and the panicky looks were almost gone. She had stopped mentioning the trip East. For a while, too, he had thought, well, this is just back the way it used to be, it isn't an affair after all, and maybe it doesn't have to end. But he knew it was only Marissa who kept them from their bed. She had been awake almost every time lately. And he had thought, Marissa, you've got more brains than both of us put together, and we ought to pay attention to the signals you send us. But then the baby had slept again, and they'd made love again.

One day she'd asked him, do you still sleep with your wife, and he had told her, yes, he did, and he wasn't sure what she thought. She'd turned away, and that new lightness he had thought he had seen drifted off, disappeared right into thin air. But she was laughing again the next day, and so he'd decided to push things just one step further, and he'd asked her if she slept with Paul. He knew it was manipulative — and therefore unkind — because he was certain she didn't sleep with him. He had his own reasons for asking. He had thought, if she's sleeping with him, as I'm sleeping with Deena, it won't be so hard for her when I leave. He was clumsy about it, too indirect, he knew, asking about him, but not really saying what he thought. He'd been ashamed of himself afterwards.

Then that night he'd stayed awake for hours, working it all out. He could see that there was something perverse about a man setting his lover up with another man before he left her. And that was what he was trying to do, wasn't it? But there were special circumstances here. First, the other man was her husband. And second, he'd probably wrecked them up to begin with. He'd been telling himself how she and Paul didn't have any relationship anyway, but that was garden-variety rationalization, pure self-conning. Here was the bottom line: he didn't know what kind of relationship they had. He didn't know why she couldn't sleep with him. He had a sense that there hadn't been time yet for them, that they had moved out here too fast, with her mother dying and the baby being born. And if that were true, he'd interrupted them, pure and simple.

So he had asked his questions with some misgiving. He would get himself through by saying, I owe her this much, but most times that sounded self-serving to him, and he would be unable to continue. One day he said to her, we can't go on forever, you know. Then he'd wanted to say, I didn't mean it to sound as cruel as it did, but he had just held his breath while they continued with their lunch. She had almost smiled. How much easier it would be, he thought, if she was the one saying these things instead of me.

"I've a vacation coming up in a couple of weeks," he had said. "We'll probably visit Deena's brother." She had just nodded, a little distracted maybe, like she was thinking. I don't do this lightly, this leaving you, he had thought. But that sounded self-serving, too, so he hadn't told her.

He dreamed of her. He figured he had the dreams because he wanted to know what would happen to her after he left. They were good dreams, and things worked out well in them. In the dreams, Amy and Paul had an elegant restaurant dinner with wine and they grew soft and romantic (and in one version they both cried a little), and at home, over a nightcap, Paul seduced her. She forgave Paul for whatever had split them: for bringing her out here, maybe, for not caring enough about her mother dying, maybe. Paul forgave her. They decided to have another baby. He knew it wasn't necessarily realistic, that there was wishful thinking involved, but it wasn't impossible, either, that it could happen that way.

When he woke from his dreams, he missed her, sometimes hoped she would leave Paul, as he once had hoped. He would have two wives again, perhaps for the rest of his life. When he was really awake, though, he would stop thinking that way.

He wished he could write her a letter. It would begin, Darling, and it would explain everything. Sometimes he thought he would leave directions that it wasn't to be read for three years or five years. He would explain that it would have been different in different times, back when people really did have mistresses, back when that was part of life. He would say he loved her. He put none of it on paper. How could he?

Once upon a time she had thought he would disappear suddenly. There one day, gone the next. That he would find some other more compelling spot to visit. Back then, she had not expected to see it coming so clearly. Now she knew that he would drift away from her slowly, day after day, little by little, past her line of sight. In the final moment before he slipped beyond the horizon, she would know: any minute now, and it will all be over. When he said, "You ought to sleep with Paul," she knew it was very close to the end. On the very last day he said to her, "I'm not your lover anymore." He held her hand, as if it were a rare and tiny object, on the palm of his hand, looking at it, running his fingers along it. "After vacation I can't come back," he said. She hadn't gone away, wouldn't go away, so now he was going away. He kissed her then, and when his hand was on the knob, the door half opened, he turned back and said, "Why don't you get a bottle of wine for dinner?"

Even that? she thought. His words chilled her. Nothing else he said had. "To celebrate, you mean? Should Paul and I toast your departure?" she asked him.

"No," he said. "I thought you could make note of our end. Make it official."

"Will you celebrate it?" she asked him, and she could feel the sharp edge of her voice trying to cut his flesh.

"Not celebrate," he said. "Just make a note of it. It needs an ending." Such reason and rationality, she had thought later. She sifted through her flute literature and played most of the afternoon. Then she wept. "Joe," she said aloud, over and over.

The next day at noon she called Julia. She began to cry as soon as she heard her sister's voice. "Julia," she managed to say through tears, "it was hard."

"Amy," her sister said, "what on earth is the matter?"

"Having a baby without her here. It was hard."

"Of course it was," Julia said.

"Mama should have been here. Mama didn't even know I was having a baby."

"I know."

"I needed help, Julia." She was unable to continue for a moment, for tears had swollen up in her throat like a child's half-finished, too-early-swallowed peppermint.

"Please don't cry," Julia said, crying herself. "I feel just awful now. I should have come, shouldn't I? I should have come and helped you. Forgive me for being so thoughtless."

"It's all right," Amy said. "I just missed Mama. It was Mama I needed and couldn't have." She had stopped crying. "Everybody dies," she said. "I just have to accept it."

"Or not think about it, like you said the other day."

"I already tried that. It's all right from time to time, but it doesn't work for very long. It doesn't last."

"Don't you have any earth mother–type friends who like to mother babies and new mothers? I have a couple of those."

Joe, she thought, earth father, recently dead, also.

"And Paul helps, doesn't he?" Julia asked.

"I don't know," she said.

"You don't know?"

Someone Takes Care of Us All. Of mothers? Of fathers?

"He helped," she said. Then added, in order to leave the topic of Paul behind and to enter the world of meaningless generalization, "You know the way men are," making laughs sound out above her tears. "Listen, Julia," Amy continued. "Should I come out there when your baby is born? I know I'm inept at child care, so I wouldn't be of any practical use, but I could come anyway."

"I'll be all right, Ames. I'm a third-time mother, remember? But why don't we get together, just to visit. Just so I can see the baby."

"Maybe I'll come out there," Amy said. "I'll think about it and let you know." They closed with more loving words than usual.

Twenty

*A*ND where were the mementos, she wondered? Why hadn't she gathered one or two, in the tradition of a lock of hair? She walked through the apartment searching for a sign that he had been there but could find none. If only he'd dropped a china teapot, smashed a treasured plate, she could pick up its pieces, say, here, see, Joe was here, he did this. Every little charm he'd brought her, those brownies, those petits fours, she'd greedily consumed. Joe, she said, a token, please.

She thought, would the library have information on postal workers that she could read, for surely she could bundle Marissa up, and they could walk the mile or so distance to the reading room. She would read about what? she asked herself as she pulled on high socks and boots. Postal regulations? History of the postal service? "How your letter travels to your friend?" Supreme foolishness, surely. She dressed Marissa warmly and went to the grocery, instead.

She still checked the calendar, keeping a running record of the ratio of days he had been there that month to days that he had not. They were losing scores she recorded. She sifted through the pages of her notebook, looking for references about what they had done, what he had said. There was almost nothing. She paused over the page that said "Bath" and turned to the next one. What secrets had she thought were in her book that she had to hide it away? There was still time, though; it was still fresh enough in her mind so that she could catch something of him, of them, and put it down.

She would be bold and daring. She took out her two pens, opened the one with the thinner point, then sat with it poised ready over the page. First, she would title it, she thought. She would write his name at the top, then things about him, about them.

Joe? Eddie? Maybe she ought to leave his name off altogether.

She recapped her pen. What did she want with souvenirs, any- way? It hadn't been a sporting event or a Broadway musical. She ripped those pages that had writing on them, one by one, from the notebook and tossed them, along with the calendar, into the trash basket beneath the desk.

Then he left a package. Although she couldn't be absolutely certain it wasn't the relief man, and that he wasn't still away on vacation. But she didn't think so. He should have been back al- ready. When she'd gotten to the door, there was nobody there, just a package — another pair of flannel pajamas from her sister — propped against the house. The truck wasn't even in sight. He must have run to get away that quickly, she thought. Now he was hiding from her. Well, all right, she thought, I can take care of myself now. I'm doing perfectly fine. She hoped the packages had stopped.

Three days later she bought a bottle of wine. She pulled the table over closer to the door, further from the stove and refrigerator, so it would seem more like a dining area, maybe, less like a kitchen. But she didn't like that. Then they'd be able to see the sheet around Marissa's crib. She pushed the table back. Candles and a tablecloth would help, she thought, and she decided they might both sit on one side of the table, because at least that way they could face the window, not the appliances. She found a dark red print tablecloth, but it reminded her of the fringed Victorian one Mrs. Martin used. She put it back in the linen closet. There was a cloth with a beige background and summer flowers on it, but it wasn't round, and it had a stain dead center. She considered putting candlesticks over the stain, but then couldn't find any.

If we had a large dark-stained oak table in a true dining room, not a kitchen, it would all work, she thought. A tablecloth of Belgian lace, silver candlesticks, and candles the color of emeralds for the occasion. Paul would gasp with pleasure at the deep color of the wine and would swirl and sniff it in the style of a true connoisseur. He would compliment her on her choice. She would cast her eyes down (coyly? virginally?) at her ecru lace gown. . . . She lifted the fabric and let the fold of the full skirt fall gently back round her legs. The candlelight threw the color of the wine wildly about the room; it dominated their hands and faces, the intricate lace of the cloth, and reflected off the platinum band on the white Worcester porcelain. He held her hand, they kissed, and he lifted her in his arms and began carrying her, with long, full strides, up the staircase.

Marissa's cry startled her. She put the bottle of wine in the very back of a cabinet, behind the extra rolls of aluminum foil and paper towels.

Paul found the maps in the closet. She had tossed them into a corner, behind the rows of boots along the back wall. His pulling the packet out was mere reflex action, she knew that. He had seen the plastic AAA bag and had thought it had fallen or been misplaced. Why would such a thing, otherwise, be on the closet floor? He picked it up, brushed some dust from it, and asked, "Where's this supposed to be?" At that point he still hadn't looked inside. Mine, she wanted to shout and snatch it from him. Wasn't this, possibly, the token she had sought?

"You can put it in a desk drawer," she said, her face down, her hands carefully inserting diaper pins into the face of a tiny stuffed doll.

By then he had slipped one of the books from the bag. "Mid-Atlantic region," he read. "Shenandoah. That was good camping there. What's this stuff for?"

She shrugged. "Nostalgia, I guess."

"We ought to go camping again," he said, tossing the packet onto the bed. "That was a lot of fun."

"What about Marissa?" she asked, but she was thinking about getting the packet hidden away again. She saw herself clutching a mass of brochures to her chest with one hand and backing out of the room, the other hand raised to ward off Paul's approach.

"Why couldn't we take her?"

"If it rains?" she asked. Joe had said they mustn't camp with a baby in the rain.

"We'll listen for weather reports so we're reasonably sure we'll have decent weather, but we can always go to a motel."

"Uh-huh," she said, now clutching Marissa, not maps, to her chest as she stood at the door.

"We don't have bottles or baby food to worry about. It'd be a little vacation for us. A change of pace." Her eyes were on the travel packet. Not tokens of Joe, really, not if she remembered how it had been: he had folded them up, put them away. "Early spring camping can be great," he continued. "Remember how connected we felt to spring because we were right there when things started coming alive?" She moved to the bed and put Marissa down at its center. She lifted the packet and let the contents slide out onto the bed. She spread the Blue Ridge map out, smoothing it open, and pointed to one spot.

"Peaks of Otter," she said. "It'll be nice there now." Up the Blue Ridge parkway, back into warmth.

"Not Virginia," he said. "I meant here."

"Here?" she asked, and she heard her own voice like the screech of a hungry baby bird.

"Well, not here, maybe, but there's supposed to be great spots on the lakes. I know a lot of people who do it. It's supposed to be quite spectacular."

"No," she said and stood, scooping Marissa into her arms and heading for the door.

He moved toward her, caught her arm in his hand. "Amy," he said, pleading almost, "people really do it. They enjoy it. That big camping store downtown has all sorts of equipment for the cold. Down sleeping bags if you want them."

"I don't want them," she said. She shook his hand off her.

"What do you want?" he said in tight, even word packages.

"I want to go home," she said. "I don't want to be here anymore. I never did." She clutched the baby under her arms, and the infant body hung in front of her own like a shield. "You wanted to be here, and you want to stay, not me. I hate it here. I have no one. Nothing." She shuddered at her own words. "Nothing," she repeated, and she saw his eyes narrow, his glance turn quickly aside.

"Aren't you getting better?" he asked.

Better! So he did think she was crazy. Did he think there was some other Amy who had felt all those things, some other Amy that they could now discard along with the kitchen garbage? It was she, not some aberration of herself, who hated this place. Was he asking her to forget how she once felt, who she had been? Wasn't it all part of her, connected to now, today, and tomorrow on a long strip that looped together and was her life? The strip was continuous, had no outside, no inside. All of it is me, she would tell him. "I hate it," she said, simply. "I didn't want to come."

. "No," he said, quietly, carefully, taking a small step toward her. "You wanted it, too. You didn't want to be out there because of your mother's death."

Well, yes, she thought, there was that, but that wasn't wanting, couldn't he see that? "Why didn't you stop me?" she shouted at him. "Why did you let us do it?" She tried to form more words but couldn't. She covered her face with her free hand, moving it awkwardly, as a child does, never really covering enough.

"Amy," he said and reached a hand to her. She stepped back. "Amy," he said again and added gently, "then let's go back, if that's what it is."

"It's too late," she said, "it's done. It's over."

Paul's fault, she had told Joe. Paul's the one who will want to stay. But what good would it do, anyway, she told herself. Mama's dead already. He had followed her as she backed into the kitchen. She thought she heard a truck in the driveway and went to the window — an oil truck was turning in their drive.

"I didn't know," he said. "You wanted to run, I wanted to run with you, that was all." She turned around, suddenly determined to keep him from advancing any closer. He hadn't moved but still stood at the opposite end of the kitchen, hands clasped behind his back. "It was a mistake," he said.

She sank into one of the kitchen chairs, the baby across her lap. "It doesn't matter," she said and shook her head rapidly back and forth with closed eyes.

"It does matter."

After a while she looked up to find he was coming closer but moving so slowly, so nearly silently, that he was already almost upon her. She closed her eyes again while he pulled a chair from the table and sat, his head bent forward into his hands. She looked down at him: his hair was thinning at the very top of his head. He wouldn't have seen it in the mirror, she thought, wouldn't know that he was growing bald, growing old. "Don't hate me for that one mistake," he said, his voice muffled behind his hands. How long till he was all bald? Would he still keep his beard when he had no hair on his head? Marissa, face down on Amy's lap, had begun to cry. Paul put a hand on the infant's back and rubbed it gently. "I don't think it's too late," he said. He had turned directly to Amy, had addressed his words softly to her. The baby cried more. He began to lift Marissa, then glanced up at Amy. For permission, she thought, turning away, closing her eyes once more. But she did not try to stop him. Paul held the baby and rocked her till she was quiet. Again he put his head down, this time resting his face on Marissa's round belly. Amy's hand hovered over the spot where scalp peeked through hair, then drew back. Marissa's hands became tangled in the thick parts of his hair, and Amy watched him unwind each tiny finger to free himself.

He looked up at Amy. "Is it too late?" he asked.

"I don't know," she said, her eyes on the pine tree outside the window. "I don't know." He stood and carried the baby to her crib.

After that, when they looked at each other, or tried to look at each other, or just passed one another, even, she would get a jumble of questions in her head, but they would get hopelessly entangled before she could ask one. "So what do you think?" sometimes seemed like a logical beginning, but after she'd said it over and over to herself, it sounded like a faded vaudeville joke.

She wanted to try to back up, to say, remember that conversation we had about us? He might say, you mean that fight? which wouldn't get them anywhere either. It was always when she got to that point that she gave up. She couldn't think of any way of referring back without either sounding silly or starting the battle anew. She wanted a way to pick up where they had left off, to say, do you remember when you said you thought it wasn't too late, well, I was wondering, do you still think that? Or there was the more positive approach: you said it wasn't too late. Then she would just wait for his response. She wouldn't plan it past that point.

She wanted to say, too, listen, about me being better, do you think I'm really better? You meant it?

And she thought of: are things still negotiable? But that sounded like real estate business.

Or: what must happen to get from here to there? She imagined she might say that as she dressed in the morning, turned only partly toward him. She would be in a lace slip (she didn't own one), and he would be on the other side of the bed, putting his belt through the loops. Both of them getting dressed for work. Somehow, in that setting, it could have happened. A business question would have been acceptable: how shall we proceed after work today?

Then she stopped thinking about backward references and decided it wasn't worth it. She hoped he would start it, that he would begin with, "So what do you think?" But even so, she was afraid she might say, again, always, "I don't know." It was no use. She tried to concentrate on other things.

She read labels on baby foods at the grocery store, comparing similar products from different companies. She bought a cookbook of baby food, a tiny grinder with a picture of a contented-looking baby on it, and three new ice trays to store baby-meal-sized portions of pureed fruits and vegetables. She would begin the conversion to solids. When the baby cried in the morning, Amy no longer carried her back to bed for breast-feeding but sat her in her infant seat and spooned watery baby cereal around and into her mouth. Marissa didn't like it, but Amy liked being up, not back in bed. Amy set the table for breakfast and called, "Breakfast, everyone," although Paul was the only person to whom that "everyone" could apply, and they all three sat down together.

"We have a guest for breakfast," Amy told Paul. She liked the new arrangement: Marissa was joining them now, rather than Amy dropping everything to meet baby demands. Paul decided to try feeding Marissa on the third day, and she blew little bits of watery rice flakes back at his Harris Tweed jacket. He put on an apron and tried again.

Paul got a ride home one night and walked in a half hour early. She was playing the flute in the bedroom and didn't hear him come in.

"Hey," he said from the doorway, startling her so that she

jumped, "that sounds good." She started to dismantle the instrument. "You're finished?" he asked her.

"Yes," she told him.

"It sounded good. Why don't you play something else for me?"
She was a little winded, she said, maybe tomorrow. She snapped the case shut.

"You ought to get back in a chamber group," he told her.

"I think I'll wait a while," she said. "Till my breath holds out better."

"You sound very good," he said. "You should get in a group."

"Do you really think so?" she asked him.

"I really do," he assured her.

He went in the kitchen and opened the refrigerator, scanning for fruit. She slid the flute back on the closet shelf and thought, what I need to do now is to pack small parts of my life into a box and send them by mail somewhere else, far away. Those little patches of worse that were in there to contrast with the better: I have no use for them anymore. Reverse the process, hand the box to the postman at the door. Thank you very much, here's who I was, you remember that, don't you? Would it be an even exchange?

She had said to Eddie, look how I'm better, look how I'm changing. Now she must tell Paul. That was what was left. Paul was ready for better.

She was ready for better: scrape the windows down, once and for all.

Paul suggested wine for dinner that evening. "Like we used to," he said. He had pulled his coat on and was ready to walk to the liquor store three blocks away.

"I've got a bottle," she said and went down on her knees at the cabinet, practically reaching her whole body inside to pull it out.

"Where'd this come from?" he asked.

"I bought it," she said. "For emergencies. In case we had a

sudden longing for wine one night." He reached into a top cabinet for wine glasses.

She wondered if he'd say it once more: you're getting better, you are better, you're fine now, everything's just fine, really OK. Maybe it was already too late. And probably that wouldn't be enough anyway: they had slammed infinite numbers of doors to reach this spot.

The wine glasses were large, and he filled their round bowls very high.

She watched the red move in warm patterns over her hand as she swirled the wine in her glass. One thing: if this were a long time ago, she would have reached out now and touched the beard, traced its shape round his face. Felt the ends of it where it lapped lightly round his lips, pushed it gently to left and right, so lips could touch only lips. She held her wine up and tried to see him through the deep red liquid. She could not.

"To Amy," he said.

"To Paul," she said, and they clinked their glasses so vigorously, the wine sloshed onto the floor, onto their fingers.

"Such exuberance," she said, "we almost broke the glasses. And we've only five left as it is." They both laughed. She licked the wine from her fingers.

She watched her own hand, illuminated, it seemed, by intermittent flashes, reach toward his face. She moved the mustache left, then right, and his fingers, wet with wine, reached for hers.